PRAISE FOR *FAITHFUL RUSLAN*

"Vladimov's particular distinction was as a dissident of immense moral courage, and as the author of *Faithful Ruslan*, one of the defining literary texts of the post-Stalin period. His life was one of constant vicissitudes, but his authority and fortitude remained firm to the end." —THE GUARDIAN

"[A] perfectionist whose writing took him much effort ... Vladimov produced a set of works that captured the mood of the times, but whose craft will ensure they survive. —THE INDEPENDENT

"Known as a writer of strong conscience ... Mr. Vladimov's best-known work, *Faithful Ruslan*, is a chilling, cynical parable of false hopes in the post-Stalin era." —NEW YORK TIMES

"Russia's political reality can be best understood through Russian fiction. Today's Russia, for instance, calls to mind *Faithful Ruslan*, a novella by dissident writer Georgi Vladimov."

—THE ST. PETERSBURG TIMES (RUSSIA)

"[An] exceptionally talented writer who has been cut down in mid-career and who is being hounded by the KGB. One reason for the persecution is his celebrated novella, *Faithful Ruslan*, which has circulated all over the country in samizdat." —TIME (1980)

FAITHFUL RUSLAN

GEORGI VLADIMOV was born Georgii Nikolaievich Volosevich in 1931 in Kharkov, Ukraine. As a child, his father was killed in World War II, and his Jewish mother was sent to the gulag in one of Stalin's anti-Semitic purges. He began using the pseudonym Vladimov when he took up journalism after graduating from law school in 1953. His first novel, *The Big Mine* appeared in 1961, drawing praise for its frank take on issues of Soviet life such as alcoholism. But government censors delayed his next book, *Three Minutes of Silence*, for years, accusing him of "perverting Soviet reality." In response, Vladimov aligned himself with Andrei Sakharov and the dissident movement, eventually becoming director of the Moscow branch of Amnesty International—a treasonous act. His work circulated in samizdat throughout, including a story called "The Dogs," which would eventually become the novel *Faithful Ruslan*. Finally published under his name in 1978 in Germany, Soviet authorities refused to let Vladimov leave the country to respond to international invitations until 1983. He thereafter remained in exile, publishing books such as *The General and His Army*, which won the Russian Booker in 1994. He did not return to Russia until 2000, when he was offered a residence in the official writers' colony near Moscow. He nonetheless continued to spend most of his time abroad, and died in Frankfurt, Germany in 2003.

MICHAEL GLENNY (1927–1990) was a British intelligence officer who quit to become a salesman for Wedgewood, which first took him to the Soviet Union. He was the first to translate Bulgakov and Solzhenitsyn into English, as well as numerous dissident authors.

THE NEVERSINK LIBRARY

I was by no means the only reader of books on board the Neversink. Several other sailors were diligent readers, though their studies did not lie in the way of belles-lettres. Their favourite authors were such as you may find at the book-stalls around Fulton Market; they were slightly physiological in their nature. My book experiences on board of the frigate proved an example of a fact which every book-lover must have experienced before me, namely, that though public libraries have an imposing air, and doubtless contain invaluable volumes, yet, somehow, the books that prove most agreeable, grateful, and companionable, are those we pick up by chance here and there; those which seem put into our hands by Providence; those which pretend to little, but abound in much. —HERMAN MELVILLE, WHITE JACKET

FAITHFUL RUSLAN

GEORGI VLADIMOV

TRANSLATION AND FOREWORD
BY MICHAEL GLENNY

MELVILLE HOUSE PUBLISHING
BROOKLYN, NEW YORK

FAITHFUL RUSLAN

Originally published in Russian by the émigré publishers Possev Verlag, Frankfurt am Main, as *Vernyi Ruslan,* by Georgi Vladimov Copyright © 1978 by Possev Verlag

Translation and Foreword copyright © 1979 by Michael Glenny

Design by Christopher King

First Melville House printing: August 2011

Melville House Publishing
145 Plymouth Street
Brooklyn, NY 11201

www.mhpbooks.com

ISBN: 978-1-935554-67-7

Printed in the United States of America
1 2 3 4 5 6 7 8 9 10

    Library of Congress Cataloging-in-Publication Data

Vladimov, Georgii, 1931-2003.
  [Vernyi Ruslan. English]
  Faithful Ruslan / Georgi Vladimov ; translated By Michael Glenny.
    p. cm.
  ISBN 978-1-935554-67-7
  I. Glenny, Michael. II. Title.
  PG3489.3.L29V413 2011
  891.73'44--dc23

                2011026231

FOREWORD TO THE FIRST ENGLISH EDITION (1979)
BY MICHAEL GLENNY

If the reading public outside the USSR has heard little of Georgi Vladimov until now, it is not from a lack of talent in this author, as this novel will show; it is due rather to the exceptional difficulty he has encountered in having his books passed by the Soviet literary censors. In a land where all media are controlled by the state and where writers must follow rules that govern not only their subject matter but even their style, Vladimov has found it harder than most other Soviet authors to get his work into print. Although his writing is remarkable for its originality, insight, honesty and ironic humor, these qualities are not enough to earn publication in the Soviet Union—in fact they can be a positive hindrance. This novel, for instance, which many Russians regard as Vladimov's masterpiece, completed in 1974, has never been printed in the USSR.

Faithful Ruslan has an unusual history, even by Soviet standards. In the years 1963–65 Vladimov wrote a short story called simply "The Dogs"; it described how a peaceful May Day procession was attacked and broken up by a pack of former prison-camp guard dogs, who mistook the procession for a column of prisoners. The story was unsigned, and for the ten years or so in which it circulated illicitly from hand to hand in typescript, readers were so impressed by its qualities that its authorship was generally ascribed to Solzhenitsyn. During those years, however, Vladimov was not content to leave the story in its original form; as the idea continued to ferment in his mind, he changed the emphasis, expanded the story to the length of a short novel, rewrote it again and again in his careful, scrupulous fashion until it had been so transformed that it was a work of altogether different character and far greater scope. At some point in this process (only the author knows when it was) he retitled his book *Faithful Ruslan*. This time he did not allow it to be passed around in *samizdat* ("self-publishing"—the Russian term for the unofficial circulation of forbidden typescripts); instead, knowing that it could never be legally published in the Soviet Union, he made arrangements for it to be printed abroad in West Germany, whither he managed to smuggle out a copy at the end of 1974. In order to conceal the fact of its relatively recent completion, at the author's request the date of the original story "The Dogs" (1963–65) was printed at the end of *Faithful Ruslan*. When this final version of the story appeared in 1975, taking up almost a complete issue of *Grani* (the émigré Russian literary journal published in Frankfurt-on-Main), it bore at last its author's name.

Georgi Vladimov was born in the Ukrainian city of Kharkov in 1931. "Vladimov" is, in fact, a pseudonym; his real name, in its full form, is Georgii Nikolaievich Volosevich, but he has always published under the name of Vladimov. His father was killed at the front in World War II; his mother was imprisoned during the final surge of Stalin's terror in 1952. Soon after graduating from the law school of Leningrad University in 1953, Vladimov began working as a journalist on a small provincial newspaper. Starting in 1954, his reviews and critical articles made their appearance in Soviet literary magazines. From 1956 to 1959 he was an editor in the prose section of the journal *Novy Mir*. One of his best pieces of criticism, published by *Novy Mir* in 1961, was a stimulating and perceptive review of J. D. Salinger's *The Catcher in the Rye*. In its July issue of the same year, *Novy Mir* also published Vladimov's first novella, called *The Big Mine*, notable for its crisp, direct style and the startling frankness (by Soviet standards) of its treatment of matters such as alcoholism.

This promising debut as a fiction writer was somewhat overshadowed by the worldwide sensation created when in 1962 *Novy Mir* printed Solzhenitsyn's *One Day in the Life of Ivan Denisovich*, which marked the emergence of a new Russian writer of towering stature and tended to eclipse all other literary topics. In more than one way, however, Solzhenitsyn's epoch-making novella provided the stimulus for Vladimov to write the story that evolved into *Faithful Ruslan*. This is only partly because Vladimov followed Solzhenitsyn in taking Stalin's infamous prison camps as his basic theme. Solzhenitsyn is rather the godfather of Vladimov's novel in a wider sense, namely that thanks to the political skill of Tvardovsky (the editor-in-chief of *Novy Mir*) in getting Solzhenitsyn's work into print, the long-standing and previously rigid taboo on the prison camps was broken. The publication of *One Day in the Life of Ivan Denisovich* opened the sluice gates that had been holding back a pent-up torrent of prison-camp literature, and Soviet magazines and publishing houses were swamped in a tidal wave of manuscripts on this subject. Very few of them were ever published, because the shock caused by Solzhenitsyn's novella alone was enough to make Khrushchev and the rest of the Soviet leadership regret even this concession to liberalism. After some delays and hesitation, a ban on the prison-camp theme was effectively reimposed, although in more ambiguous and less draconian form than under Stalin.

The greater part of this flood of prison-camp literature was the work of actual survivors of the camps, written from bitter personal experience. At the same time the topic itself (and the possibility, since the appearance of *Ivan Denisovich*, that more of such writing might get published) also stimulated the creative imagination of writers of a generation younger than Solzhenitsyn, writers whose age had spared them from becoming the direct victims of Stalin's terror but who had suffered from it through the murder or brutal incarceration of parents or close relatives.

One such writer was Georgi Vladimov, who started work on "The Dogs" in 1963, at the time when the shock effect of Solzhenitsyn's revelations was at its height. It took him nearly two years to finish this short story, partly because he was simultaneously busy earning his living as a journalist and critic, but also because Vladimov is a fastidious and painstaking literary craftsman. In 1965 (the year after Khrushchev's fall from power), he offered it for publication, but despite the support of several distinguished writers who were very impressed by it, the time had passed when a story like this could have any chance of being published in the USSR.

Indeed the mere fact of having shown such a "subversive" work to a number of editors had a dire effect on Vladimov's career in general, and it was another four years before Tvardovsky found it possible to publish Vladimov's next story in *Novy Mir*'s issue for July 1969. This is the moving, masterfully written story, entitled "Three Minutes Silence," of a confused but honest young man in search of an identity in a society that chiefly lives by false values. It is also the last of Vladimov's fiction to have been published in the Soviet Union; since then this gifted and original writer has been banned from print in his own country. Although he has written other works, he has been writing them—in the expressive Russian phrase—"for the desk drawer."

After enduring this humiliating and frustrating professional ostracism for nearly eight years, the last straw for Vladimov was the moment when, having never been outside the USSR in his life, he was refused an exit visa for a meeting with his Norwegian publisher. On October 10, 1977, in a bitter, scathing letter to the Executive Board of the Union of Soviet Writers, he poured out his scorn for the members of that board, servile bureaucrats who "manage" Soviet literature under orders from the Communist Party leadership; enclosed with the letter, Vladimov sent back his membership card of the Writer's Union.* At the same time he announced that he had joined the Moscow branch of Amnesty International, a move regarded by the Soviet authorities as tantamount to treason.

That those same Soviet cultural bureaucrats would regard *Faithful Ruslan* as, if anything, even more treasonable, will come as no surprise after reading the novel; in its ironic and telling fashion it is much more than just another angle on the prison camps: functioning at more than one level of meaning, it is a very subtle yet penetrating critique of the moral squalor inherent in Soviet communism—and which, by implication, it shares with all totalitarian systems.

---

*An abridged English translation of Vladimov's letter was published in the *New York Review of Books*, issue of May 4, 1978, p. 47.

The eponymous "Ruslan" of Vladimov's novel is one of the guard dogs that were (and to a lesser extent still are) employed as auxiliaries to the human guards in Soviet prison camps. *Faithful Ruslan* was written for a Soviet Russian audience, and Vladimov naturally assumed in his readers a prior knowledge of recent Soviet history, which he therefore did not need to spell out. This framework, of dates, events, personalities and statistics may not, however, be quite so familiar to English-speaking readers, and since many key allusions in the story will not make much sense without a certain minimum of background information, a brief outline of the relevant facts may be helpful.

Prison camps, or "corrective-labor camps" as they are officially termed, have existed in the USSR since the earliest years of Soviet rule.* From relatively modest beginnings in 1919–20, the scope of the prison-camp system was vastly expanded during the 1930s to accommodate the ever-growing numbers of the real or imagined objectors to Stalin's drastic policies, until by the end of that decade it probably housed some twelve million prisoners, the vast majority of them not only innocent of any crime but innocent of any form of opposition to the regime; they were merely digits in the arithmetic of a calculated rule of terror.†

At the end of World War II there was a huge new influx into the camps, when, as a deliberate act of retributive policy, Stalin imprisoned en masse all returning Soviet prisoners of war and all Soviet civilians who had been deported by force to work in Germany during the war. Thereafter until Stalin's death in 1953, his increasingly paranoid mind created

---

*The most complete available account of the Soviet prison-camp system is to be found in A. Solzhenitsyn's *The Gulag Archipelago* (New York: Harper & Row, 1974).
†Robert Conquest, *The Great Terror*, rev. ed. (New York: Macmillan, 1973), p. 708.

new categories of "enemies of the people" to be packed off to the camps: writers and intellectuals, Jews, Old Bolsheviks, former political refugees from Nazi Germany, religious believers, anyone having the most innocent contact with foreigners—the list was interminable.

So evil and grossly inhuman was Stalin's system of terror that among the first priorities of his successors was to stop the flow of new prisoners, then to release the inmates and dismantle the whole prison-camp system. This, to his great credit, is what Khrushchev largely succeeded in doing after his denunciation of Stalin to the 20th Congress of the Soviet Communist Party in 1956. Over the next twelve months, an estimated eight million prisoners were released from the camps, and about six million who had perished there were "posthumously rehabilitated."* As part of this process, the monstrous organization (known by its Russian acronym as "Gulag") that had kept them all behind barbed wire was almost entirely liquidated.

Although *Faithful Ruslan* does not always keep to a straight chronological sequence, making occasional uses of flashback, the main narrative covers an actual timespan of about eight or nine months. It starts in the winter of 1956–57, when Khrushchev's policy of closing the prison camps and freeing the prisoners is being put into effect. The story opens, in fact, on the day after all the prisoners in a particular camp have been sent home and most of the guard troops have been demobilized. The locale of the story is a prison camp somewhere amid the vast forests of Siberia; it is sited at a distance of perhaps two or three miles from a small- to medium-sized

---

*R. Medvedev and Z. Medvedev, *Khrushchev: The Years in Power* (New York: 1976), p. 20.

town on the Trans-Siberian Railroad, along which new prisoners were shipped into the camp in special prison trains, and the lumber, felled and cut by the prisoners as part of the corrective-labor regime, was shipped out. Temperatures in Siberia can be extreme: while very hot in the short summer, the thermometer can frequently hit -50 °C in winter. Soviet prison regulations stated that at temperatures below -40 °C prisoners could not be made to do outdoor work, but this rule was not always observed by prison-camp commandants.

The troops used to guard and escort the prisoners were not subordinate to the Ministry of Defense, as were the rest of the armed forces, but were under the authority of the Ministry of State Security, an immensely powerful organization that thus disposed of a very considerable private army, enjoying special privileges of pay, leave, pensions, etc. The security troops were also fortunate in that they were never sent to fight in the front line; on the other hand, a large proportion of them were obliged to endure the same extreme climatic conditions suffered by the inmates of the Siberian camps.

Within a prison camp, duties were divided between the internal guard, responsible for security inside the double-barbed-wire perimeter, and the external or escort guard, whose job it was to watch over the prisoners when they were taken to their work sites outside the camp. The latter was regarded as the harder and more responsible task; each soldier of the escort guard was a trained dog-handler, to whom was assigned a specially bred and schooled guard dog. For some years these animals were generally crossbred, mainly German shepherd crossed with various long-haired Russian hunting breeds (short-haired breeds, such as Doberman pinschers or boxers, could not survive in the Siberian climate), but in time it was found that the most suitable breed was the *Kavkazskaya ovcharka* or Caucasian sheepdog, so that from World War II onward only this type of dog was bred for the prison service and frontier patrolling. "Ruslan" is of this breed.

All guard troops were armed with the standard Soviet infantry close-combat weapon, the Degtaryov 9-mm submachine gun, with an air-cooled barrel and a drum-type magazine holding seventy-two rounds. The watchtowers around the camp's perimeter were manned by the internal guard and armed with the regular Soviet Army medium machine gun, the Maxim 7.62-mm with belt feed and a fluted water-cooled barrel—a very accurate weapon with a high rate of fire. All guards were under standing orders to shoot to kill any living creature that entered the No-Go Zone between the inner and outer perimeter fences.

The prisoners in "Ruslan's" camp would have been a mixture of real criminals with totally innocent politicals, the latter greatly predominating in numbers. The criminal prisoners generally despised and bullied the politicals, and this fact was cynically exploited by the prison authorities; by giving minor privileges to the criminal element, they were utilized to keep the politicals in subjection. Another universally applied policy was to blackmail or bribe prisoners into acting as informers; in any group, such as a work team or a camp hut, at least one inmate was bound to be working as an informer to report on any subversive talk or behavior. These men were naturally feared and loathed by their fellow prisoners, and it was by no means uncommon for informers to be beaten up, mutilated or murdered when their role was discovered. A striking episode in *Faithful Ruslan* depicts the fate of just such an informer.

During the period covered by the novel, a prisoner could be serving a sentence of anything from five to twenty-five years. It was also very common for sentences to be extended as punishment for some real or trumped-up breach of regulations, so that a prisoner might serve for double the original length of his sentence, or more, without leaving the camps. The ex-prisoner who is one of the main characters in *Faithful Ruslan*—Vladimov gives him no name but simply calls him "the Shabby Man"—belonged to the large category of camp inmates, several millions of them, who were automatically imprisoned on being repatriated to the USSR from German prisoner-of-war camps in 1945. Formally, his release from the Soviet prison camp was due to a blanket "amnesty" extended by Khrushchev to all such ex-POWs; this term was distinct from the procedure known as "rehabilitation," which was granted to civilians or soldiers who had been imprisoned for a specifically political offense under Stalin (the "offense" was, of course, fictitious and no more than a pretext by which the security forces fulfilled their quota of arrests). Rehabilitation carried with it certain privileges, such as a right to proper housing for victim and family, and a right to reinstatement in a job appropriate to his qualifications. Prisoners like "the Shabby Man" who were merely amnestied had no such rights of restitution; when freed, they had to fend for themselves, find whatever work was available for a man who might have lost his health or his skills, and reestablish a home without any special state assistance at a time when there was still a drastic housing shortage due to war damage. Thanks to yet another rotten deal from life's deck of cards, "the Shabby Man" therefore finds himself in the worst possible category of the released prisoners; it is important for the reader to be aware of this in order to understand the motivation for his behavior in the story.

Any further explanation would usurp the author's rights. *Faithful Ruslan* must from here on speak for itself, and it is to be hoped that the reader will gain as much pleasure from reading it as did the translator from putting it into English.

MICHAEL GLENNY

FAITHFUL RUSLAN

1

ALL NIGHT IT HOWLED, THE LAMPS CREAKING and swinging, the outside latch rattling; then toward morning it subsided, grew quiet and Master came. He sat on a stool and smoked, waiting for Ruslan to finish his broth. Master had brought his submachine gun with him and hung it on a hook in the corner of the kennel, which meant that there was to be duty, after a long time in which there had been none; therefore he must eat without hurrying, but without lingering either.

Today the feed included a large marrowbone, so enticing that he felt like taking it away immediately into a corner and pushing it under the bedding. Later he would be able to gnaw at it in the proper way—in the dark and alone. With Master there, however, he felt shy of pulling it out of the feeding bowl, and contented himself with stripping all the meat off it, just in case; experience told him that when he came back the bone might not be there. Carefully pushing it aside with his nose, he lapped up the fatty juice and had started gulping down the lumps of warm, meaty stew, dropping them and picking them up again, when suddenly Master shifted on his seat and asked impatiently:

"Ready?"

As he stood up, he dropped his cigarette butt, which fell

into the feeding bowl with a hiss. This had never happened before, but Ruslan did nothing to show that it surprised or upset him. He merely looked up at Master and wagged his heavy tail in a token of gratitude for the food and of his readiness to earn it by a spell of duty. He refrained from even glancing at the bone, instead only hastily lapped up some more juice. And with that he was quite ready.

"O.K., let's go."

As Master held out his collar, Ruslan willingly stretched out his neck to take it; he wriggled his ears in response to the touch of his master's hands as they fastened the buckle, tested to see that it was not too tight and secured the spring clip to the ring. Master wound some of the leash around his hand and fastened the very end of it to his belt, so that throughout their spell of duty they were joined together and could not lose one another. Then with his free hand he threw up his gun, caught it by the sling and hung it over his shoulder with the sweating barrel pointing downward. Ruslan took up his usual position beside Master's left leg.

They walked down the gloomy corridor into which all the kennel doors opened. Behind their heavy wire mesh gleamed moist, slanting eyes; the dogs who had not yet been fed whined and butted the grilles with their bony foreheads, while at the far end, one dog, burning with envy, was giving tongue in a sobbing bark. Ruslan felt proud that today he was the first to be taken out on duty.

The moment the outer door was opened he was dazzled by a blinding white light, and recoiled with a start, blinking and growling.

"Come on!" said Master, giving the leash a jerk. "You've had it easy for too long, you idle brute. What's the matter—never seen snow before?"

So that was what had been howling all night. It had settled like a thick, fluffy blanket all over the deserted parade ground, on the roofs of the barracks, storehouses and garages, forming white hats on top of all the lampposts and covering the benches grouped around a trash can. Snow had fallen many times in Ruslan's lifetime, but it always came as a shock to him. He knew that the masters called it "snow," but to him it was not something that had a particular name; to Ruslan it was simply whiteness. Because of it, everything changed and lost its normal meaning, the world to which his eyes and nose were accustomed became void and dull, and all tracks were hidden. The only thing visible was a clear double line made by his master's boots, leading from the kitchen to the doorway. Next moment the whiteness struck his nostrils, and he was overcome with nervous excitement; he dipped his muzzle into it up to the eyebrows, plowed a furrow and crammed his mouth full with it. Snorting, he even gave a silly, cheerful sort of bark, which meant roughly: "You fraud, I know you!" Master was not holding him in, but had unwound the leash to its full length. With a white beard and white eyelashes, Ruslan would sometimes hang back, sometimes run ahead; keyed up, he avidly gulped the air and sniffed around in vain for scents.

This was the reason why he committed a minor blunder—he failed to look about him in the regulation manner required when on duty. Yet something alerted him; he pricked up his ears and stopped, rooted to the spot, feeling a vague sense of unease. To the right were the bare poles and the barbed wire; beyond that were the deserted fields and the dark, jagged-topped edge of the forest; to the left were the same poles and wire and another stretch of field, but dotted with huts—squat and low, almost like underground storage-cellars, built of untrimmed logs that had turned black with age. And as always their little windows stared at him, covered now with hoarfrost and as blank as blind eyes. Everything was in place, nothing had moved, but a strange, unprecedented silence had settled on the world; his master's footsteps were muffled as though he were walking on a layer of felt bedding. Strangely, too, there were no eyes peering out of those windows; no one was showing any curiosity to see what was going on in the world (a habit in which people were no different from dogs!). What was more, the huts themselves looked oddly flat, as though merely painted on a white background, and not a sound came out of them. It was as if the horde of noisy, smelly people who lived in them had all suddenly died in the night.

But if they had died, he would surely have sensed it, and if not he, then some of the other dogs would undoubtedly have dreamed about it and waked up the others with their barking. They're not here, thought Ruslan. Where can they have gone? He immediately felt ashamed at being so slow-witted. They hadn't died—they had escaped. He began to quiver with excitement, breathing hotly and noisily; he wanted to pull at the leash and drag Master after him, as had happened on those rare and unusual occasions when they had run for miles and finally caught their quarry—and never once had they failed to catch him! This had marked the start of his real life in the Service; it was the best thing that Ruslan had ever known.

Yet not everything fitted into that rare and unusual pattern either. He knew the word "escape," and could even distinguish between "single escape" and "group escape," but at such times there had always been a great deal of noise and nervous bustle; for some reason the masters had shouted at each other a lot and had lashed out at the dogs for no reason at all, while the dogs themselves, confused and jittery, had always started fighting and snapping at each other and could not be calmed down until the chase began. He had never known silence like this before, and it aroused the most frightening suspicions. Not only had all the inmates of the huts broken out in a mass escape, but all the masters seemed to have gone after them, too, and in such a hurry that they had not even had time to take the dogs with them—and without the dogs, of course, what sort of a chase could there be? So now just the two of them, Ruslan and his master, had to find all the runaways and chase them back—the whole stinking, howling, maddened herd of them.

He felt a wave of fear that made the pit of his stomach turn cold, and he ran forward to look up at Master's face. Something was wrong with his master: he was walking with a wholly unaccustomed stoop, glancing morosely from side to side, and his right hand was not holding the sling of his submachine gun, as it always did, but was thrust into the pocket of his greatcoat. It occurred to Ruslan that Master looked as if he had a cold feeling in the pit of his stomach, too, which in view of the task facing them today was not surprising. He pressed against Master's greatcoat and rubbed him with his shoulder, which meant that he understood everything and was ready for anything, even to die if need be. Ruslan had not yet had to face death himself, but he had seen men and dogs die. There was nothing more terrible, but if he was with Master, it was another matter: that he could stand. This time, however, Master did not notice Ruslan touching him, did not give him a reassuring pat on the head in return, as he always did, and this was a really bad sign.

Suddenly he saw something which made his hackles

rise and a growl start rumbling in his throat. Although not distinguished for his good eyesight—aware of this failing, he did his utmost to make up for it by diligence and a keen nose—Ruslan immediately caught sight of the main gates of the camp as Master and he passed through the small wicket gate into the outer perimeter. The gates looked so strange that Ruslan could not believe his eyes: they were wide open, creaking in the wind on their long rusty hinges, yet no one was running toward them with shouts and rifle fire to hasten to shut them. What was more, the other gates, on the outer side of the perimeter zone, were never supposed to be opened at the same time as the inner gates, and now they were open, too; the white road between the inner and outer perimeter fences simply led straight out of the camp, no longer fenced in, no longer blocked by the bars of the gate, but it simply faded away toward the forest on the dark horizon....

And what on earth had happened to the watch-tower? It had been completely blinded: one searchlight was covered in snow and pointing straight down, the other, its broken glass looking like a jagged grin, was dangling by a wire. Gone were the white sheepskin coat and the fur hat, gone, too, the long, ribbed machine-gun barrel that was always aimed downward. The faded red banner above the gates was still there, but someone had torn it so that it was hanging down in disgraceful tatters, blown about by the wind. That strip of red cloth, with its mysterious white markings, had always had a special significance for Ruslan: etched into his mind was the memory of the scene when, on dark evenings after work, in every kind of weather—frost, snowstorm or pouring rain—flanked by masters and dogs, the column of prisoners had halted in front of the banner, when both searchlights had suddenly flared into life and their two, long, smoky beams had joined at the banner; as it hung there, blazing across the entire width of the gateway, the prisoners would involuntarily jerk their heads up and stare, shivering, at its dazzling white markings. Ruslan was not able to interpret the full, hidden wisdom of those markings,* but they somehow stung his eyes until tears came, and he, too, would feel a sudden tremor, a thrill of sadness mixed with an excitement that produced a delicious sinking feeling inside him.

All this damage and vandalism stupefied Ruslan. He was amazed at the impudence of the escaping prisoners, who must have been quite convinced that no one would chase them. It was as if they had known it all in advance—that snow would fall and cover all their tracks, that it was difficult for a dog to work in the cold. But worst of all was the fact that they had made no particular effort to conceal their intentions: he well remembered how the prisoners had behaved throughout those last, incomprehensible days when the dogs had languished with nothing to do and only Ruslan's master had come—without his gun—to feed them and take them out to stretch their legs a little in the exercise yard. It had been puzzling in the extreme. The prisoners had wandered freely around the accommodation zone in herds, had played their squeaky accordions, bawled songs, and even started to tease the dogs; their extraordinary behavior had made no sense at all at the time. But how had the masters failed to notice anything, when literally all the dogs had sensed that something was amiss and had gnawed at their bedding in angry frustration?

Ruslan did not blame his master or reproach him. He was

---

*The usual wording on these banners was as follows: "LABOR IN THE USSR IS A MATTER OF HONOR, OF GLORY, OF PROWESS AND HEROISM. J. STALIN." (Author's note.)

no longer young, and he knew that masters sometimes made mistakes. But then, they were allowed to. It was not permitted, however, to dogs and prisoners, who always had to answer for their mistakes and often for the masters' mistakes, too. If his master ever committed a blunder, Ruslan knew that he must share the responsibility with him and help him to put it right at any cost. As he thought how skillfully the runaways had fooled his master, he began working himself up into the right frame of mind for the job in hand and stimulating his bad temper to the point where he got genuinely angry. His bad temper was colored yellow. The sky and the snow took on a yellow tinge, the faces of the escaping prisoners looked yellow as they glanced around in terror on the run, and the soles of their boots flashed like yellow specks. As he vividly imagined the scene, Ruslan burst uncontrollably into furious barking, tugged at the broad rawhide leash and pulled Master after him toward the gates.

"Hey, what the hell's the matter with you?" Master could hardly keep on his feet. He pulled Ruslan toward him and did his usual trick to calm him down: hauled him up by the collar so that his front paws dangled in the air. Unable even to growl, Ruslan could only wheeze. "Where are you going in such a hurry? Afraid you won't be in time to get to heaven? Don't suppose they need your kind there!" Then he let him down, unfastened the spring clip, coiled up the leash and put it into his pocket. "Off you go, now. Just keep on straight ahead; you can't go wrong."

He pointed along the white road and into the fields. This could only mean one thing: "Scent, Ruslan." This was work that Ruslan could do without any orders. The trouble was that he could not pick up so much as the hint of a scent.

He gave Master a quick, anxious glance that was close

to despair, lowered his head and began plowing the snow with his nose as he made a circle in the prescribed manner. It smelled of dried-out moldering grass, mice and ashes—but not of people. Without pausing, he made a second and wider circle. Again nothing. It was so long since the prisoners had passed this way that it was stupid even to try to pick up any meaningful scent. And he never allowed himself to play false by setting off at random, pretending he had picked up a real scent, and then putting on a hysterical act as though his master had made a mistake. In any case, Master could not have made a mistake: it was as clear as could be that the prisoners had walked out through the gates, as free as air. Soon he grew exhausted, feeling as if his guts had somehow dropped out, and he sat heavily down in the snow on his behind. With his steaming tongue lolling to one side, blinking guiltily, twitching his ears, Ruslan honestly admitted that he was helpless.

Master was looking at him, his mouth twisted into an unpleasant grimace. Nor did Ruslan find any sympathy in his eyes, those two entrancing round saucers suffused with dull blue—they showed only coldness and mockery. It made him want to flatten himself on the ground and crawl on his belly, although he knew that entreaties or complaints were useless. Whatever those beloved eyes wanted to be done was always done, no matter how much Ruslan might whine or even lick his boots, smeared with pungent-smelling boot polish. There had been a time when Rush had tried licking Master's boots, but then one day he had seen a man lick them—and it had done the man no good.

"Want to try it farther away?" Master asked. "Or would you rather be here, near the guardhouse?" He looked at the gates and slowly unslung his submachine gun. "Makes no difference; here will do just as well."

Ruslan was seized by a fit of shivering and an uncontrollable yawn pulled his jaws wide open, but he mastered himself and stood up. He could not do otherwise. When the worst happens, an animal always takes it standing up. He realized that it had come to him now, on this white day, that it had already come a minute ago and there was no avoiding what was to follow. No one was to blame. Whose fault was it that he had ceased *to understand what was happening?*

He knew well what occurred whenever a dog stopped understanding what was happening. No amount of previous good service could save him. His first recollection of it had been with Rex, a very keen and experienced dog, a favorite of the masters, whom Ruslan in his young days had fiercely envied. The day of Rex's fall had been a very ordinary day, and none of the dogs had felt any sort of presentiment: as usual the escort detail had taken over the column of prisoners from the camp guard, as usual the prisoners had been counted and recounted, and the customary words of warning were spoken. But hardly had they marched out of the gates when one of the prisoners had suddenly uttered a wild scream as though he had been bitten, and had taken to his heels. He must have been mad, because there was nowhere for him to go, out in the open fields and in full view of everyone. He never did get anywhere, for almost before his shriek had died away there came a rattle of gunfire from three or four barrels, in which the machine gunner on the watch-tower also joined. Yes, strange as it may seem, those two-legged creatures were sometimes capable of such stupidity! The prisoner's foolishness, however, greatly confused Rex, who was walking alongside him, and who ought to have been alert enough to have sensed what the man was going to do; even if he had committed a momentary lapse of attention, he should then have hurled himself in pursuit and immediately brought him down. Yet Rex, bemused by the prisoner's behavior, merely sat down with his tongue hanging out, allowing three more men to break ranks and to start waving their arms and shouting at the masters. They were instantly driven back into line with gun butts, helped by several dogs, but Rex did not even join them in this. He had completely stopped understanding what was happening. He bounded over to the man on the ground—who was not even groaning any longer—and sank his teeth into his right arm. It was such a stupid thing to do that Rex did not growl as he did it but only whined pathetically. Rex's master dragged him off and, in front of everyone, kicked him hard in the stomach. For the rest of the day Rex was allowed to continue doing escort duty, but all the dogs knew that Rex had committed an inexcusable blunder, and Rex himself understood this better than any of them. After duty he suffered for his shame all evening; he lay as though sick, with his nose in a corner of the kennel, and refused to touch his food. That night he started giving tongue with a howl that drove all the other dogs mad with dread foreboding, and not one of them closed an eye in sleep. Next morning Rex's master came for him, and none of his whining and bootlicking had any effect. He was led out into the fields beyond the wire; they all heard the short burst of automatic fire, and Rex did not return. He did not quite disappear altogether—for a few days longer his presence could be smelled in the camp, and at a short distance from the road the dogs could see his bloated flanks, surrounded by carrion crows, to remind them of Rex's terrible mistake. In time, all trace of him vanished. Rex's kennel was washed out with soap, his feeding bowl and bedding were changed, another nameplate was hung on the door and a new arrival moved in—Amur, a young dog whose career was just beginning.

Sooner or later it happened to all of them. Some lost their "nose" or went blind from old age; others got too familiar with the prisoners and began to make little concessions to them; others, from overlong service, were afflicted by a terrible clouding of the mind that made them growl and attack their own masters. The end was always the same—they all went the way of Rex, beyond the wire. There had only been one exception, when a dog called Buran had died in his own kennel. When Buran's back had been broken from a blow with an iron pipe during a struggle with two escaping prisoners, the masters had carried him home from the forest on a greatcoat, had stroked him and tickled him behind the ear, saying, "Good dog, Buran.... Well done, Buran, you got him!" They did not know what to give him to eat, but that evening they put something into his food from which he died at once in convulsions.

It was thus the custom that a dog's life in the Service always ended in death at the hands of his master. In all his eight years spent in the camp, Ruslan had never ceased to be aware that one day this would happen to him, too. It frightened him and gave him nightmares, from which he would wake up to the sound of his own eerie-sounding moans; gradually, though, he came to terms with the idea, realizing that although it could not be avoided altogether, it could be put off by showing enough zeal and exerting oneself to the utmost. He accepted his impending fate as the natural culmination of his life in the Service, as something that was proper, right and honorable—just like the Service itself. No dog, after all, would have wished for any other end—such as being chased out of the camp gates, for instance, and left to an existence of begging and scrounging alongside the mangy mongrels who lurked around the kitchen trash chute, gobbling scraps of rotten meat. The thought of it horrified Ruslan.

Therefore he did not crawl, did not whine for mercy or try to run away. If his master could have seen Ruslan's eyes—yellow, unblinking, with deep, clearly defined pupils, dark as burnished gun-barrels—he would have found not a trace in them of hatred, suffering or entreaty, but only humble expectation. His master, however, was looking somewhere above the top of Ruslan's head, and he raised the muzzle of his submachine gun skyward. Something behind Ruslan was preventing him from opening fire. Ruslan looked around and saw what it was. He had noticed it earlier out of the corner of his eye, had listened with half an ear to its rumbling and clanking, but had forced himself to pay no attention, being wholly occupied in looking for a scent.

A tractor was coming up the white road to the camp. It was crawling slowly, looking as though it had been a part of these snowy fields and grayish-white sky for so long that the landscape was unimaginable without it. Nosing forward with two big, staring eyes on either side of its ribbed snout, all black soot and streaming exhaust, it was pulling a sledge behind it. On the sledge, making it sway and occasionally slither off the roadway, was a vast, reddish-brown object far bigger than the tractor itself; as it came closer, the thing turned out to be a railroad freight car without wheels, lashed onto the sledge with rusty hawsers.

Ruslan growled and moved out of the way. Tractors were nothing new to him. They were used to haul logs away from the lumber-felling site in the forest, and his experience of them had been wholly bad. The black smoke of their exhaust had caused him to lose his sense of smell for a long time, which had made him the most helpless creature on earth. What was more, the men who drove the tractors were "free workers," a tribe of people who were alien and strange to Ruslan; they wandered around everywhere unescorted and they treated the masters without proper respect. They also used to make their own way to the work site, so that by the time the column of prisoners was just marching into the forest, the free workers were already there and horsing around. A nasty bunch.

The tractor crawled forward and halted, but did not stop roaring; something inside it gave an indignant howl, and through the noise the driver bawled a greeting to Ruslan's master. Ruslan was amazed by this. As far as he could remember, no other biped had ever spoken to his master like this:

"Hi there, soldier!"

The mere look of the driver was infuriating, too: an ugly, shiny, crimson-red mug slashed by a thick-lipped, fire-breathing maw that gaped in a cheeky grin from ear to ear. His cap, which he did not take off to Master, failed to cover a blond forelock that stuck wetly to his forehead, something that was unthinkable for a prisoner, as was the way he fired off a whole string of questions at Ruslan's master:

"You weren't waiting for me, were you? What? Can't you hear what I'm saying? I've brought this boxcar for you; where d'you want me to put the damn thing? Or can't you speak for your boss? Are you checking passes? Sorry, forgot to bring mine. Maybe you won't let me out again, eh?"

With this he burst into a horrible, disgusting guffaw, as he leaned out of the door and put his foot, clad in a felt boot, onto the track. Master made no reply to his laughter or his questions. Ruslan knew that he would not reply. This habit of the masters' never ceased to thrill Ruslan: whenever a prisoner asked them a question, they would either answer only after a long pause or not answer at all, but simply stare at him with a cold, impassive and sarcastic look. It did not take long before the eager questioner lowered his eyes and drew his head down between his shoulders; sometimes the man's face would break out in a cold sweat. The masters caused the prisoners no harm by this treatment, yet their mere silence, combined with that stare, produced the same effect as a clenched fist raised to a man's nose or the rattle of a rifle bolt. At first Ruslan thought that masters were born with this magic ability, but later he noticed that they answered each other readily enough, and if they were asked a question by the Chief Master, whom they addressed as "Comr'd Cap'n P'mission Tspeak," they answered very promptly and held their hands straight down the sides of their pants. Hence he suspected that the masters, too, were specially taught how to behave toward prisoners—just like the dogs, in fact!

"What are you looking so miserable for?" asked the driver. He did not lower his eyes, did not hunch his head between his shoulders or break into a sweat, but merely put on a sympathetic expression. "Sorry to finish your spell in the service, are you? Don't like the idea of starting life all over again, I suppose. Don't worry, you'll find your feet. Only I shouldn't go back to your old village, though, if I were you. Heard about the plenum of the Central Committee? Not much to eat back on the farm these days, I hear."

"Keep going," said Master. "You talk too much." He did not, however, stand aside for the tractor, and kept holding his gun firmly against his chest with both hands.

"Sure thing," the driver agreed. "It's a fact—can't seem to stop my tongue from wagging. How can I help it, though, if it itches?"

"I'd give you something to stop it itching," said Master.

The driver roared with laughter.

"You kill me, soldier!... Hey, but you look good with that gun. Had your picture taken for a souvenir? You'd better; otherwise your girl won't have you. All those sluts want to see is a gun, they don't care who's behind it." Master did not answer, and the driver expostulated: "See here—where the hell d'you want me to put this boxcar?"

"Put it where you like. It's no business of mine."

"Well, you're standing in for the boss around here, aren't you?"

"For all I care, you can chop it up for firewood. Why have you brought it here, anyway? Aren't you going to live in the huts?"

"Hell, no! I'd rather live in a tent."

Master shrugged his shoulders impatiently.

"Please yourself."

The driver nodded, still grinning all over his face, climbed back into the cab and was about to shut the door when he caught sight of Ruslan. He seemed to remember something; his forehead betrayed signs of thought and a furrow of sympathy appeared on it.

"You gonna shoot that dog? Thought at first maybe you were giving it some training. I saw you as I was driving up, and I wondered why the hell you were training the dog when it was time to put it out to grass. So you've got to bump it off.... Look, maybe you don't have to do it. Couldn't you leave him behind for us? A dog like that must be worth a fortune. He could guard our stuff for us."

"He'd guard it all right," said Master, "but you wouldn't like the way he does it."

The driver looked at Ruslan with respect.

"Couldn't we retrain him?"

"Not this one. All the dogs that could be taught new tricks have been retrained already."

"I see." The driver shook his head sadly. "They sure have given you a shit job, soldier—shooting dogs. Well, it's all in the line of duty, I suppose. What a reward for good service—nine grams of lead in the back of the neck. But why do only the dogs get that treatment? You served your time, too, didn't you?"

"Are you going to drive on?" asked Master.

"O.K.," said the driver, "I'm on my way."

Their glances met head-on: Master's rigid and ice-cold, the driver's somewhat abashed but still carelessly cheerful. The tractor roared and enveloped itself in clouds of black smoke, Master stepped reluctantly aside, but the tractor did not go straight ahead; instead it gave a jerk, swiveled its nose away from the gates and crawled diagonally across the ground, churning up the soil of the No-Go zone between the inner and outer perimeter fences.

An instant flash of anger sent Ruslan across the road in one bound. The reddish-brown color of the boxcar and the squeak of the sledge runners as they forced a dirty track through the snow combined to whip him into a frenzy, so that he could only see one thing clearly—the driver's big, bony elbow sticking out through the window of the cab door; he longed to sink his teeth into it and bite through to the bone. Ruslan growled and whined, dripping saliva and looking imploringly at his master, begging him to say, "Get!" He was bound to give the command: Master's face had turned pale and he had clenched his teeth—Ruslan was sure he would hear it any moment now, flashing out like a red spark and seeming not to come from the mouth but from the hand flung forward to point: "Get him, Ruslan! Get!"

Then the real business of the Service would begin. The joy of obeying orders, the furious headlong dash, the feinting leaps from side to side—and the Enemy would dither in confusion, not knowing whether to run or to stand and defend himself. Then the final leap, forepaws tucked into the chest, when you would knock him to the ground and fall with him, growling furiously into his distorted face, but you would only seize his right arm, because he was gripping something in his right hand and you would hang on and hang on, listening to him shouting and thrashing about, and a warm, thick, intoxicating liquid would fill your mouth—until Master forcibly dragged you off by the collar. Only then did you start to feel all the blows and wounds you had received.... The time was long past when they had given him a piece of meat or a biscuit for doing this, and even then he had taken it more out of politeness than as a reward, because he was in any case too strung up to be able to eat at such moments. Nor was there any need for a reward when later, back in camp, in front of the sullen ranks of prisoners, he was urged to attack and harass the captured prisoner, who no longer resisted but could only shriek pathetically, although this time Ruslan ripped his clothes more than his body. The greatest reward for Service was the Service itself—yet strangely enough, for all their intelligence, the masters never understood that and thought they had to offer the dog something by way of encouragement. Somewhere at the very edge of his consciousness, in a yellow mist, there still lodged the black thought of what his master had intended to do to him, but he was even prepared to accept that, provided he could first have this final reward of the Service, provided Master would only say, "Get!" He felt strong and fearless enough to leap up onto the clanking tracks, drag the Enemy out of his cab and wipe the grin off his cheeky face, the grin that even his master's all-powerful look had been unable to efface.

His jaws convulsed with impatience, Ruslan shook his head from side to side and whined, but Master still delayed and would not shout "Get!" There then occurred the terrible, shameful thing that should never have been done. With a hoarse rumble, the tractor's snout nudged a fence pole as though sniffing it, and gave a savage roar. It did not move, but the caterpillar tracks churned and churned and the pole creaked in response; it tried desperately to stay upright, but was already keeling over slightly, tightening the twanging strands of wire, and then suddenly it snapped with a bang like a round of gunfire. Only the wire now held it up and prevented it from falling over completely, but the snout crawled relentlessly forward and strand by strand the wire fell into the snow. The tracks crushed it into the ground, wound it into tangled plaits, and then the sledge runners crawled over it with a protesting screech. When the pole reappeared behind the sledge, it was lying flat, like a man spread-eagled on the ground.

Grunting with satisfaction, the tractor halted inside the No-Go zone. The driver climbed out to inspect his handiwork. He, too, looked satisfied and bawled out to Master:

"What would you do without me, soldier? You ought to learn to do a job like mine. And all you can do is shoot dogs."

In its wide-open quilted jacket, his chest was a perfect target for a shot; but Master had already rested his submachine gun in the crook of his elbow, extracted his cigarette case from inside his greatcoat and was tapping a cigarette on the lid. He looked at the picture on the lid, which he had engraved himself with a shoemaker's awl, and grinned. He liked looking at his own work and always smiled as he did so, and whenever he showed it to other masters they would almost fall over with raucous laughter. Having put the cigarette case away, with the same sarcastic grin he watched the tractor making its terrible way toward the inner line of fencing; there it again attacked a pole, which proved to be somewhat tougher, so that the tractor had to butt the pole several times after backing away to get a run at it.

When that pole collapsed, too, Master finally turned to Ruslan as though seeing him for the first time.

"Still here, you stupid brute? I thought I told you to get lost." He stretched out his hand that held the smoking cigarette, again pointing down the road and toward the forest. "And I don't ever want to see you again—got it?"

It was not that Ruslan could not understand the order; he would not have accepted it for anything in the world. For the first time he was being ordered to go in quite the wrong direction. A human had gone up to the wire and broken it and ... he had been forgiven, whereas others had been attacked without warning for trying to do the same thing. That was why he felt such a violent hatred for the grinning driver, whose shameless impertinence had saved not only Ruslan's life but the lives of all the other dogs who were still in the kennels and awaiting their turn.

However, he obeyed and went. Having gone a little way he stopped to hear whether his master was following him, and looked around. Master was walking back into the camp through the gap made by the tractor, holding his submachine gun by its sling so that the butt almost trailed along in the snow. As he stared at his stooped back, Ruslan suddenly had a feeling that his master no longer needed either his dog or his gun. In despair and shame he wanted to sit down in the snow, raise his head toward the yellowish-gray disk of the sun and howl to it out of his boundless misery. The end of his life in the Service had turned out to be even worse than he had always feared: he had been taken outside the wire simply to be kicked out, to be condemned to a life of undignified beggary alongside those lousy mongrels that he despised with all his soul and whom he hardly considered to be dogs. Why? What for? He had done nothing bad enough to warrant this special, unique form of punishment.

But an order from Master was an order, even if it was his last, so Ruslan trotted away along the white road toward the dark, jagged skyline.

He knew that he would follow that route for a long, long way—maybe for a whole day—through mile after mile of forest, and that at twilight, on a high hill, he would see through the trees the scattered, flickering lights of the town. In the town there would be wooden sidewalks smelling of pitch through the snow, and fences as high as the wooden barrier on the obstacle course at the training school; the town would smell of smoke, and delicious aromas would be coming out of the low, squat little houses, from which scarcely a gleam of light escaped past the thick shutters. Further on it would smell of trains and a different sort of smoke, and eventually he would reach the little square in front of the station. In the middle of the square there was something that Ruslan had also first seen at the training school: two men, who were the color of an aluminum feeding bowl and who did not move, had for some reason climbed up onto a pedestal and were acting: one, without a hat, had stretched out his arm and opened his mouth, as though he had just thrown a stick and was saying, "Fetch!" while the other, in a peaked cap, was not pointing anywhere but had thrust his hand inside his uniform jacket; his whole look made it clear that whatever was being fetched should be brought to him.

In a siding at the station there would be a broad platform, which was easily reached in one bound from the ground. The long ribbons of the tracks, curving and intertwining, flowed past the station, in daylight sometimes tinged blue and in the evening pink. But the tracks that led up to *the* platform were always rusty and came to a stop where the platform ended; their ends were turned upward and supported a black beam with a lantern on top of it, which always shone red for the arrival of the train they were waiting for. That train was sometimes green with slanting bars on the windows, sometimes red and completely closed up without so much as a chink in the blank wooden sides. This was the end of Ruslan's route—the only one he knew.

He was running at a steady, unhurried trot, but then a sudden thought came to him and he quickened his pace. He had finally realized why he had been sent away: he was meant to be there, on the platform, when the red lantern was lit and the trainload of escaped prisoners would slowly steam into the siding.

2

NEXT MORNING THE RAILROAD MEN AT THE station saw a sight that probably would have surprised them if they had not understood its real meaning. About twenty dogs had gathered on the siding platform and were pacing up and down it or sitting down and barking in chorus at the passing trains. The timbre of their voices was clearly of solid metal. These dogs were almost all of the same coloring: a black stripe down the back divided the broad forehead in two and gave it a look of sullen menace, while the short ears and muzzle added to the impression of ferocity; the color of the flanks gradually shaded off from a steely, bluish-gray to rust-red or an incandescent orange, and the long hairs hanging down from the belly were shot with a shade that might have been called "the color of dawn." Dawn-colored, too, was the thick ruff around the throat, the heavy, crescent-shaped tail and the big, muscular paws. The beasts were handsome enough to be worth admiring at close quarters, but no one dared go up to them on the platform, because informed people knew that it might be much more difficult to get off that platform again.

As the hours passed and the trains passed—red freight trains and green expresses—the dogs' voices became shriller, the metal in them grew noticeably less thick and by twilight was as thin as tinplate. Fewer and fewer dogs paced the platform, more and more frequently they sat or lay down, staring dully at the tracks as the narrow strips of steel turned pink. Having waited on the platform in vain for their train, when darkness fell they gathered together, jumped down to ground level in a pack and dispersed into the streets of the town.

The same scene was repeated on the following days, but an attentive observer might have noticed that day by day fewer dogs came, that they left earlier and that cracks could be detected in the metal of their voices. Soon they fell silent altogether, and the five or six dogs who still kept to the schedule no longer barked or whined at passersby, merely sitting out their hours of duty in subdued passivity.

In the town itself, their appearance caused some alarm at first. There was something too menacing in the zeal with which they patrolled the streets, padding through them at a steady gait with their steaming, pale-mauve tongues lolling out of gaping mouths. Yet not once did they ever touch anybody. Soon people noticed how the dogs gathered into groups as though to hold a sort of conference, frequently glancing over their shoulders and keeping outsiders out of their circle; it was obvious that they lived their own, separate existence and were not going to interfere in other people's lives. They never noticed children or women, even when one of these occasionally bumped into a dog by mistake, but merely showed surprise at this strange object moving through space. Men alone attracted their attention, and after a while it was men who provided the dogs with a definite occupation: they would follow men whenever they went anywhere on foot—visiting, shopping or to work. When they saw a pedestrian and spotted at half a block's distance that he belonged to the male sex, one or another of the dogs would break away from the pack and take up his station a little way behind him. Having escorted him to his destination the dog would return, asking nothing in reward. Whenever a person threw them something edible, the dog would growl and turn aside, convulsively gulping down the sudden flow of saliva. Nobody knew what they lived on; this, too, was a concern that they revealed to no one. There was only one disturbing feature of their behavior: they did not like it when more than three men formed into a group. A party of three was the legal limit in Russian prison camps, but fortunately in the cold winter of Siberia larger gatherings did not occur very often. Gradually the people got used to the dogs, and the dogs in turn presumably grew accustomed to the town; at any rate, they showed no sign of wanting to leave it.

The only one who could not get used to town life was Ruslan; in any case, he had no time to spare for such things. Each morning he would set out along the white road to the camp and sit for hours outside the barbed wire. He had a great many important things to tell Master: that the train had not come yet, but that when it did come at least one of the dogs would certainly be on duty to meet it; that in general the dogs had settled down fairly well for the time being and were keeping together ... and a few other more trivial matters. It never occurred to Ruslan to worry about how he would communicate all this; somehow his master had always managed to grasp whatever Ruslan was trying to convey. He was worried and upset by something different, however—namely, what was happening to the camp. Many more fence poles had been knocked down, huge ugly holes and openings in the wire gaped between the poles that were still standing, and some strange newcomers had lit bonfires alongside the huts. They were unloading bricks from trucks and stacking them in piles, though they seemed to be doing it very casually and in between other activities, on which they preferred to spend more time, such as wrestling in the snow, lounging around and smoking for an hour or so at a time, or singing in chorus while seated on logs—sitting, in fact, on those same sacred fence poles! They took special pleasure in doing body searches on the women, slapping them on the seat of the pants or the chest, and while they were being frisked, the women roared with laughter or squealed like stuck pigs. None of this was anything like the life the real prisoners had led, and Ruslan began to feel an ever-growing fondness for those runaways. He would, he thought, forgive them for their stupid escape if only they would come back and would stand again in beautiful straight ranks with the masters and the dogs posted alongside them.

He very much wanted to go into the camp and have a good bark at these intruders, as a reminder that the camp did not belong to them and they had no right to run things according to *their* rules. But Master had forbidden him to pass through the wire, and only he could lift that ban. Twilight was falling, and still his master had not shown up. Not once had Ruslan picked up his scent or sniffed that beloved, manly smell—a mixture of rifle oil, tobacco and strong, well-scrubbed youth. All masters smelled like that, but Ruslan's master also liked to put on eau de cologne, which he bought at the officers' canteen, and besides that there was an entire bouquet that belonged to him alone, to his *character*. Ruslan knew well that humans differed from one another in character as much as dogs did. That was why each person smelled differently; you only had to take one sniff and there was no doubt about their character. His master, for instance, to judge by that bouquet, was perhaps not particularly brave, but in compensation he was totally without pity;

he was not, perhaps, overly clever, but on the other hand he never trusted anyone; his friends, perhaps, were not all that fond of him, but he made up for that by being quite prepared to shoot any one of them if the Service should ever require it of him. Knowing all this about his master, Ruslan could vividly imagine how he was feeling there in the camp among all those strangers, how he must suspect them and hate them, how his mind must be occupied with thoughts of catching and bringing back the runaway prisoners and how to punish the other masters for letting them escape. And all the while the only creature who could help him in this was sitting close by, just waiting to be called! In Ruslan's conception, his master was great, all-powerful, endowed with rare qualities—and with only one weakness: he was permanently in need of Ruslan's help. Otherwise what was the point of coming out to the camp every day, growing numb with sitting in the cold for hours and suffering the pangs of hunger?

For since that morning when he had been fed for the last time, he had not managed to procure much to eat. There was a burning sensation in his stomach, nausea was wearing him out to the point of faintness, and it was becoming more and more difficult to make the daily journey to the camp and back. Yet he had still taken no food from strange hands nor picked up anything from the ground.

Some secret, hateful enemy had put a bakery on his route, and Ruslan had to make his way through a thick, intoxicating smell that poured out of the doors every time they opened or shut, and this slowed him down. One day a woman came out of those doors and threw him the scraps of bread that the baker had given her as make-weight, Ruslan felt as if he had run straight up against a brick wall. He hardly had the strength to turn around and snarl.

"Bet you he won't take it," said the man who had come out with the woman. "That's a camp dog; they've been specially trained."

"Why? Is he afraid of being poisoned? But I'm eating it and nothing's happened to me!" With a kindly, tender expression she took a bite out of the loaf and chewed it, smacking her lips, "You see, doggy, I'm all right. What a silly dog you are!"

Ruslan looked away with indifference. He knew that trick, too: they took a bite and they came to no harm because they knew the right bit of the food to eat, but then if you ate some, your mouth would burn like fire and your whole belly would be turned inside out.

"Told you so," said the man.

Picking up the scraps, he held them with malicious glee right under Ruslan's nose. It never occurred to the stupid tease that if a dog refused food from a woman, a creature of no account, he was even less likely to take it from a man. It only aroused his suspicions. Ruslan followed the man home—and remembered the house.

Ruslan was saved by an unexpected thought that had been dormant in his memory for years but that now awoke and came to the surface—namely, that the only safe thing for him to eat was live food. Anything that was running, jumping or flying around could not have been tampered with by humans, and therefore could not have been poisoned; otherwise it would not be alive. From those far-off days when he had chased prisoners, he still had memories of animal tracks leading away from the forest paths, of bloodstained feathers, lumps of fur, bones—the remnants of other animals' prey. He tested himself on his next journey to the camp, and he was not mistaken. He turned off the path, plunged deep into the forest and within a minute he became a hunter. As though he had been doing it all his life, he immediately learned how to sniff out the runs that field mice made for themselves under the snow and to thrust his paw through the snow at the very place where a mouse was running or taking refuge. This rather meager game did not satisfy his hunger altogether, but it calmed his anxiety and inspired hope. And it enabled him to go on with his duties.

In other respects, though, things were very bad indeed. How could it be otherwise for a dog accustomed to sleeping in the warmth on clean bedding, used to being washed and combed, to having his claws trimmed, to having ointment applied to any little wounds or scratches? Deprived of all this, he soon dropped to an extreme of carelessness to which no tramp, homeless from birth, would ever sink. A tramp would never sleep in the middle of the street, and still less under the wheel of a stationary truck—which Ruslan did, and only a miracle saved him from being crushed. A tramp would avoid trying to warm himself against a heap of locomotive cinders; like a fool Ruslan did this, too, and for several days afterward he shed handfuls of his thick coat, his most reliable defense against cold and parasites, while his paws became a mass of sores, burns and cuts. Each day he grew shabbier and more emaciated, until he became repellent even to himself. Yet his eyes burned all the brighter with the unquenchable yellow fire of fanatical devotion, and every morning, having checked that a squad of dogs was on guard duty at the station platform, he would set off for the camp.

In all this time, none of the other dogs came with him. On the very first day, released from their kennels, they searched the camp high and low and found that their masters had left the place long ago, and that their only hope of seeing them again was to follow Ruslan's tracks leading to the railroad station. Ruslan was luckier than all the others, because his master was still in the camp. Ruslan knew this not so much by scent as by some superinstinct, by some conviction that he could not explain but that never deceived him—just as he had been right in following his instinct to go hunting for live game.

Ruslan dared not even think what would happen if his master were to go away like the rest. Then, no doubt, life would not be worth living ... because, on the whole, things were working out very badly. Certainly the duties of the Service were still being carried out—hunger had not yet made the dogs neglect them—but for some time now, whenever Ruslan met the other dogs they gave him sullen looks and avoided him, and when he approached a pack of them they would immediately disperse. What was more, some of them were not looking as emaciated as he was; no doubt they were less squeamish about eating carrion or garbage, and perhaps—how terrible even to suspect such a thing!—one or two of them had committed the greatest sin of all: they had sought civilian jobs in backyards, had been taken on and were now calmly accepting food *from strangers*! Had they not learned, had they forgotten, that if not today then they would be poisoned tomorrow—but whenever it might be, they would surely be poisoned?

His suspicions were confirmed. One day he happened to meet Alma; they bumped into each other nose to nose at the corner of two fences, and both were disconcerted by the encounter. He had not expected to see her looking so well-fed, cheerful and overflowing with some private joy. He remembered that Alma had long since stopped reporting for duty on the platform. Alma was surprised, too, but she immediately pretended that she didn't know him. Behind her there came running out of a gateway a smooth-haired, bowlegged male dog, coal black with white rings around his eyes, who ran off alongside her down the street. And Alma allowed this freak to give her a playful bite on the shoulder. She must have told him something as they were going along, because the black dog turned around toward Ruslan with his ugly, fat muzzle and impudently gnashed his teeth. He was actually threatening him—now that he was at respectable distance and under the protection of his female friend! Ruslan turned aside in contempt and went on his way.

Alma had refused to recognize him! Yet only the spring before last the masters had brought them together in a corner of the exercise yard, releasing them temporarily from all duties of the Service in favor of the other, special sort of service, to which they attached great importance. Even their names were changed during that time: the masters called them Bride and Bridegroom. Ruslan never found out whether anything came of that spell of Service, nor did he see Alma for a long time afterward, but the thing they had done together made them feel unusually close; later when they met on duty they were drawn to one another as closely as their leashes would allow, and they showed their liking and affection in every possible way. He hoped that they would be coupled again, but the masters decided otherwise: another dog was brought to her from somewhere else. For the first time in his life Ruslan felt that he wanted to bite one of his own kind to death, but he never met the other dog and never even learned his name.

As for this civilian dog, with his ugly, white-ringed eyes—he looked so miserable and repulsive that Ruslan had no wish to have anything to do with him.

On another occasion he picked up the trace of Djulbars, the senior dog. The trail led him to a muddy, smelly gap under a gate and into a courtyard that was festooned with laundry and piled high with firewood. Ruslan was simply dumbfounded to see Djulbars lying on a filthy old doormat beside a stack of firewood—looking just as if he were guarding it! From Ruslan's point of view, guarding this silly heap of wood made as much sense as guarding the water in a river or the sky overhead; it possessed no value, because only *people* were of any value. And though all Djulbars had to do was to lie and snooze beside the stack of firewood, this fiercest of the fierce, this thug of a dog, with a muzzle that was furrowed with scars, had adopted his new role so completely that he got up, wagging his tail and smirking obsequiously. In fact to say that he was wagging his tail was an understatement—he was positively thrashing about alongside the firewood, groveling in a frenzy of servility. And for whose benefit was all this performance? For some little runt of a man in a sheepskin jerkin, who was puttering about with a contraption of two wheels and an engine, which smelled disgustingly of gasoline and oil fumes. More than anything else this underfed weakling with his sunken cheeks looked like a prisoner, and a long-term prisoner at that—but to treat him as a master...!

Indeed, if this puny little man had realized what sort of a creature he had acquired in Djulbars, he would not have been tinkering with his motorcycle, but would have hastily grabbed a crowbar instead. Djulbars was notorious for biting whatever crossed his path, whether it was another dog, a prisoner or anything; he regarded any day as wasted in which he did not draw blood. A prisoner did not have to step out of line—if he so much as tripped or stumbled with exhaustion (a dog can always tell whether a man infringes the rules intentionally) Djulbars would seize him at once, without even uttering a warning growl. His cherished dream was to bite his own master, and he succeeded in carrying it out, with the excuse that his master had trodden on his paw. It was a serious moment; all the dogs expected that the swine would at last be dispatched to join Rex, and even Djulbars himself expected no better, but it must be admitted that he behaved remarkably: when his master came to him next morning all bandaged up, Djulbars greeted him as though nothing had happened and made a great show of limping up and down his kennel just to prove how lame he was. And he got away with it, even earning three days' leave. Presumably the masters either thought he was in the right or he was so valuable that without him the Service would collapse. He was, after all, an example to all the other dogs, being invariably rated "best in aggression" and "best in mistrust of strangers." Who could have suspected that Djulbars would ever be able to behave like such a creep and wag his tail to a stranger?

Ruslan approached and lay down facing him, staring ferociously into the eyes of this renegade. Although taken unawares, Djulbars did not seem particularly embarrassed. He trotted around the firewood stack a couple more times and yawned, showing his black, ribbed palate—an object of pride, the sign of a fierce, indefatigable biter. After yawning so hard and pleasurably that tears even started to his piglike eyes (one of which no longer opened fully, the result of a wound), he closed his jaws and his blackish-mauve lips, at the same time managing to twist his scarred muzzle into a grimace of sympathy. He was depressed to see what a state Ruslan was in—his wasted body and the anguish of his mind.

"Why get so neurotic?" asked the turncoat. "We've got

to live, old man. Think I like having to creep to that decrepit old fool? But if I didn't, he'd stop feeding me and kick me out. This isn't the camp, you know, where you got your rations and that was that. Here, if you don't wag your tail a bit, you don't eat."

"Have you given up the Service for *this?*" said the furious, incorruptible Ruslan.

"Hey, you be careful what you're saying! I report for duty with the best of them."

It was true. He always came to the platform, and sometimes twice a day. How could he fail to come, when his fangs itched so? When the train came there would be plenty of work for his teeth to do.

"Look, if you're honest with yourself"—now the renegade went over to the attack—"is it for real, this 'duty' of yours? Who told us to go and do it? How do you know whether the Service will ever come back again?"

Ruslan countered:

"How can you say that? Of course it'll come back! And when it does there'll be no mercy for dogs like you."

"Don't you worry about us! We'll be the first to answer the call. Because when it does come, you will have died of starvation, and even if you survive, you won't have the strength left to work. But look at me—there's solid flesh on these bones and I'm in great shape!"

The devotee of the Service closed his eyes. He no longer had the strength to keep up this wrangling. Strangely, he admitted the force of Djulbars's argument and realized that it might, in fact, be their salvation. He couldn't help remembering that this traitor had once rescued them all and saved them from certain death. Ruslan stood up and strolled out of the yard. In the gateway a noise made him turn around:

having put on the required show of guarding the firewood, the dog who had once gained full marks for "aggression and mistrust" had flopped comfortably down on his soft mat. As he stepped over the threshold of the gate, this dedicated zealot fastidiously shook the dust off his paws. Ruslan did not know—and do we literate humans know it any better?—that the first step on the road to destruction always takes the form of self-righteously crossing some threshold.

On that same day he also learned a great deal more that it would have been better for him not to know. Nearly all the dogs had sought a place in some backyard, they had been taken in and fed, and while waiting for the next feed they had managed to show what they could do. Some had started by raiding hen coops, which was easy enough, while others had gone after bigger livestock. Dick, who had succeeded in devouring half a piglet before he was caught, now wore a permanent scar from an iron rod—and on his muzzle, where he could not lick it properly. Trigger had literally brought about his own punishment: while trying to pull a piece of meat straight out of a boiling saucepan, he had upset it all over himself, so that he lost all the hair on half his head and his chest, in which state he had been kicked out of the door. Another dog, Breechblock, had admittedly been successful in running away with a goose in his teeth, but how long would a goose last him, and how could he go back when his new master threatened him with a poker as soon as he came in sight? At one household, which welcomed any dog who appeared, they took in two bitches, Era and Cartridge, an inseparable pair who began by fighting each other over a male who had laid claim to both of them, and then, having made up, they attacked the dog together and would have killed him if they had not been pulled off just in time. They, too, were thrown out. And what of those who were not thrown out because they did not ask or were not taken in? Thunder, having decided that he would fend for himself, found the garbage cans at the station restaurant, ate his fill of tainted meat and was now lying in a nearby ditch, silent and stiff, covered with lime. Stupid Asa thought she would hunt for cats—no great sin, and one for which Ruslan would have forgiven her, having himself tasted mouse—but she had no experience of cats and did not even know that one must never, on any account—but never!—drive this beast into a corner, and in a flash the cat's claws had scratched her across the eyes. She killed the cat, but one eye started watering and the other festered, so that she could hardly see and was going mad with pain. It was all bad, very bad. And the worst of it was not that they had ceased waiting, but that they had ceased to have faith.

NUMBED AND DEPRESSED BY ALL THESE DISASTERS, Ruslan lay with eyes closed, stretched across the sidewalk. The passersby thought he was dying. On such occasions, mankind divides itself into two sorts: one sort walks around you with wary compassion; the other sort, of sterner fiber, simply walks over you. He was unable to notice either sort, being absorbed by the pain that was burning his stomach and his gums, which he had smeared with snow. Lately he had often taken to eating snow, driven to it by thirst and by the nausea that came with extreme hunger. Suddenly he remembered that he had not been to the camp today; he was appalled that he had only just thought of this and had, in fact, failed to go for a long time. The thought was as terrible as the anticipation of some unknown punishment. Hunger was affecting his memory. He made an effort to recall the smell of the man who had offered him the scraps of bread, but he could only summon up the smell of bread—and all that he could see, behind closed eyes, was bread. When he tried to envision his kennel, the only thing that swam into his consciousness was the marrow bone that he had left in his feeding bowl, with a damp, yellow cigarette butt alongside it. The thought of it, however, made him get up from the sidewalk.

I must go, thought Ruslan. There's so much news to tell Master! It was terrible to find how unwilling he was to set off on the long journey. Twilight was approaching, and he would have to come back in the dark, or worse still, by moonlight. In the dark he could hardly see anything, but moonlight drove him out of his mind, because it always awoke in him a host of vague but menacing forebodings. In this respect Ruslan was a wholly typical dog, the true descendant of that primeval Dog who was driven by fear of darkness and hatred of moonlight toward the fire inside Man's cave and forced to exchange his freedom for loyalty. To cheer himself up, Ruslan began thinking about the marrowbone, which his master had perhaps not thrown away but had kept for him. Somehow, though, he could not really believe in it; it had never happened before that an abandoned piece of food ever came back, unless you hid it or buried it at once. And he thought of the sin he had committed by forgetting his duties; no doubt that damned moon was his punishment for this failure. Every sin, even the smallest, was always punished: this was a rule he had well and truly learned in his canine lifetime, and he had never known there to be an exception to it.

He had reached the end of the town's main street, with its high, solid fences and houses with tiny, little, blank windows that seemed to have been made for any purpose except looking out of them. At this point Ruslan was stopped by a thought that came into his mind—a recollection of something that had happened not long ago but that had already grown blurred in his memory. Yet it would not allow him to go on and it filled him with a certain vague presentiment—not sad, but pleasant. He whined and circled around and around on the spot, like a puppy discovering his own tail for the first time, and suddenly he stood quite still with his paws spread wide on the ground. After standing like this for several moments, he lowered his head and slowly trotted back, not sure whether or not to believe his instinct. Here was the place that he had run past in such haste, preoccupied with his thoughts. Admittedly it was on the far side of the street, but he should have been able to pick up Master's scent at that distance. He had, it seemed, been driven into town by car—curse that stinking rubber, curse that gasoline!—but he had got out and stamped his feet while they handed him his suitcase and duffel bag. There was no way of sniffing what was in the suitcase, which was coated with some sort of smelly glue, while the duffel bag contained clean laundry and soap (lilac-smelling, from the officers' canteen), also Vaseline, smeared on preserving jars to make them airtight. Here he had lit a cigarette; the match still smelled of smoke and his fingers. Then he had picked up his suitcase and slung the bag over his shoulder, so that all smells stopped and the only clue was Master's footsteps, firmly imprinted in the snow. Now Ruslan could not go wrong. Master's legs were slightly bandy and perhaps a little short for his height, but he trod hard, putting down the whole of his boot sole at once, as though carrying a heavy weight. Today he was wearing his very best pair of leather boots—which were admittedly the same that all masters wore—but then his feet inside them were wrapped in footcloths and they (as we have already explained) smelled of Master's special character. It was a good thing, too, that his footsteps did not weave around among the tracks made by other people—Master never did like to take a wavering course—but went straight ahead without any deviations to either side.

Now the pedestrians shied away from Ruslan; they took him, in his frenzy of love, for a mad dog that had broken loose—and he really looked terrifying: so emaciated that his ribs showed, a yellow film over his eyes, panting hoarsely and with his loose collar clinking as he ran headlong with frightening single-mindedness toward his unknown goal. At the station his way was barred by a slowly maneuvering truck; Ruslan dived underneath it, hurting his back, but the scent made him ignore the pain and drew him on, through the doors and into the warmth and noise of the station building. There, on the slushy floor among the sweat-soaked felt boots, rotten sacking, rawhide straps, gobs of spittle, sodden cigarette butts and dirty, exhausted bodies, the thread of the scent was broken off—the thread that had been fastened to his nostrils and that he had been following like a bull running after the ring through its nose. He tried in vain to pick up its vital, magnetic pull, but there were food smells in the air, too, and their delicious, spicy odors drove him absolutely crazy. Then suddenly he heard his master's voice, that inimitable, godlike voice—and although it was not calling him, it was somewhere nearby. He flew straight as an arrow in that direction, over benches and sacks, ready to knock down anybody who would not let him reach his master.

He was obliged, however, to contain his joy. As he burst into the restaurant, he was about to bark: "I'm here! Here

I am!" when he saw that Master was not alone but was sitting at a table and talking to another person, and Ruslan did not dare approach him. Standing timidly by the wall, he stared at Master and his companion—a fussy little man with a pink, sweaty bald patch on the top of his head, wearing an extremely shabby overcoat, with a green scarf draped over his chest that no doubt concealed either a dirty shirt or the absence of a shirt. Ruslan compared the two, and the comparison was wholly in favor of his young, strong, slim, utterly splendid master. He would have looked even more splendid if he had not forgotten to put on his epaulets and had not been sitting with his uniform collar unbuttoned and his sleeves rolled up. Even so, his face was magnificent, godlike, with beautiful, godlike, saucer-round eyes, and he held himself in a magnificent and godlike way. The man facing him, on the other hand, was simply repulsive, with a pair of watery little eyes, an idiotic habit of giggling for no reason and of scratching his unshaven cheek with all five fingers as he did so. Both of them, it was true, gave off a smell that was not just unpleasant but sickening, and the source of this loathsome reek, as Ruslan suspected, was contained in the little decanter full of a clear, waterlike liquid. With a little effort, however, he was able to convince himself that his master smelled much less, in fact hardly at all, whereas the Shabby Man exuded an intolerable stench. Ruslan had already taken a dislike to the Shabby Man, because the fact that he was there prevented Ruslan from dashing up to Master, but especially because he was talking to Master in a strangely careless and disrespectful manner, failing to lower his eyes and, what was worse, with an obvious grin on his face. Just like that tractor driver.

"I see you had to stay behind for quite a while, Sergeant," said the Shabby Man. "The others cleared off long ago."

He kept addressing Master as "Sergeant," whereas his real name was Corporal, and oddly enough Master seemed to prefer this new name. Ruslan didn't like it at all. He liked names that contained the letter *R*; he liked his own name because it began with *R*, and in Corporal there were no less than two of them, and they both made a lovely growling sound, whereas the single *R* in Sergeant was hardly sounded at all.

Master did not answer immediately, because he did not like doing two things at once, so before replying he finished filling two glasses from the decanter—first one for himself, then another for the Shabby Man.

"There was a reason for it."

"You don't have to tell me, if it's a secret."

"Secret? No, it's no secret any longer. I was guarding the camp records."

"The re-ecords, eh?" drawled the Shabby Man. "You mean all the files on us? And aren't they being guarded any longer, now that you've gone?"

"Not likely. They've been sealed up and taken away."

"I see. But what for, Sergeant?"

"Whad'ya mean, 'what for'?"

"Well, why do they have to be guarded and sealed at all? They should just be put in a stove and burned—and good riddance. And all that 'secret' stuff, too. Into the stove with it, till there's nothing but ashes."

Master gave him a pitying look.

"What are you, a kid? Or have you gone crazy? Don't you know those records are to be kept forever?"

"There's no such thing as forever, Sergeant. You're an intelligent man, you ought to know that."

Master sighed and picked up his glass. Immediately the Shabby Man picked up his; this was all he had been waiting for.

"Here's luck," said Master.

The Shabby Man stretched out his glass toward him, but Master beat him to it, raised his own slightly higher so that they could not clink glasses and quickly tipped it into his mouth. The Shabby Man slowly drew his hand back and drank. Then they both took a sip of yellow stuff out of mugs and stuck their forks into the food. Ruslan swallowed his saliva and couldn't bring himself to look away.

"You still haven't answered my question, Sergeant," the Shabby Man reminded him.

Again Ruslan's master sighed.

"What more can I say? I treat you like an intelligent person and you talk like a kid. I'll try and give you an example to make it clearer. You've seen young kids collecting bugs and butterflies and so on, haven't you? Well, when they've caught 'em, they stick a pin through the bugs and write something about 'em in a notebook. That's what 'keeping forever' is like."

"What's 'forever' about it? In a year or so there'll be nothing left of that bug except a bit of dust. Well, let's say in ten years."

"No, it won't be just a bit of dust!" Master raised his finger. "'Cause it's all been written down about it in a notebook. So that bug still exists. You may think it's gone, but it hasn't—it's still there."

Ruslan looked reproachfully at the Shabby Man. Master's finger should have convinced him, but he just went on grinning and scratching his cheek.

"So we are just so many bugs, is that it?"

"That's right," said Master. Clasping his elbows with his hands, he leaned on the table and looked at his companion with a kindly smile. "You've flown away, spreading your wings and going wherever you please—but you're all still there in those records. At any moment you can be picked up again and questioned. If anyone has anything on his conscience, or has tried to duck out of sight for some reason, it's all there..."

"But we've been declared not guilty and given a free pardon, after all..."

"Think so? Well, you can go on thinking it if you like. But I'd advise you to look at it a bit differently if I were you. You should tell yourself you've been... temporarily released. Got it? You've been temporarily entrusted with your freedom. Besides, that way you'll appreciate it more. Because I've noticed the way you've been acting, now you're free. Hanging around bars, getting a bit fond of drinking, aren't you? Now back in camp your head was clear as a bell and your liver was in good shape. Isn't that so?"

"Well, I suppose you might say so." The Shabby Man seemed to be agreeing with him. "But in that case, what is there worth knowing about us? We're pretty well washed up. The stuffing's coming out of us. Now take them, fr'instance"—he nodded toward the people sitting at the two nearby tables—"what d'you know about them?"

"Don't worry, we'll get them, too, if need be. There's plenty about them in the records."

The Shabby Man also leaned on the table, and for a long time they stared into each other's eyes, grinning cheerfully.

"By the way," said the Shabby Man. "I noticed your finger was twitching, Sergeant. Your hands are shaking, even more than mine. You're twitching all over, brother. Is that 'forever,' too?"

Master frowned, took his hands off the table and reached for the decanter. He poured an equal amount into each glass and held the decanter's mouth over the Shabby Man's glass so that he would get the last drops. The Shabby Man watched his hand. Master noticed this and shook the decanter, although there was nothing left in it to shake out.

They drained their glasses again and sipped some more yellow stuff, after which they grew more friendly, and the Shabby Man no doubt felt embarrassed at his question.

"But you can't say I was a monster," said Master. "Did I ever once touch you, for instance?"

"No, you never touched me."

"There you are. And the reason was that you'd got the message. If the gov'ment thought you ought to be punished, that means there was a reason for it. They don't punish people for nothing. Once you understood that, then it's O.K.—I'm human, and I treat you like a human being, too. That's my rule. Of course, if I'm ordered to lay hands on you, that's another matter. I took the oath of allegiance when I joined the army, didn't I? But if I get no such order... Get me?"

"I get you, brother."

"O.K., then. But the ones we roughed up, they were the ones who never got that message. They just didn't understand people like you and me. But you and I—we understood each other, isn't that right? Right. That's why I sat down with you here."

Either the Shabby Man could finally stand Master's look no longer or he was tired of arguing with him, but for whatever reason, he lowered his eyes.

Ruslan, too, was growing tired of waiting for Master to notice him amid the noise and bustle of the restaurant. People going in and out jostled him, and he pressed himself pathetically against the wall until he thought of a good way to occupy himself and to be of use to his master: he would guard his suitcase and bag and the greatcoat thrown on top of them. With a gentle, inward reproach to Master for being careless, he lay down beside the luggage with dignity, taking up the position that always inspires us with respect for a four-footed sentry and prevents us not merely from approaching him but from coming closer to him than one pace. The position was also a good one in that it allowed him to watch his master's face. He was slightly disturbed by the drops of sweat that had broken out on Master's forehead and upper lip, but even so it was a splendid, godlike face.

Ruslan had long since observed that, despite their obvious differences, all masters' faces were in some respects alike. A face might be broad or narrow, might be pale or dark, but all of them invariably had a slightly cleft chin, tightly closed lips, a small nose, prominent cheekbones and honest, piercing eyes from which it was hard to discern whether they were angry or laughing, but which could keep up a stare for a long time and could command without using words. Faces like this could only belong to the most superior breed of bipeds, to the most intelligent, priceless and select race, but he had always been curious to know one thing about them: were these faces purposely selected for the Service or was it the Service itself that made them look as they did? With dogs it was simpler: Toby, a black dog with one white ear, who spent all his time hanging around the kitchen, had belonged to the Service as much as any of them, otherwise he would not have been kept on strength, but for the whole of his mysterious career in the Service, he had never grown an inch in size, had never changed his coloring and had never changed in character—always remaining a scrounger and a windbag; he would even bark at a fly, whereas to prisoners—through the wire—he simply wagged his tail. The dogs, of course, were specially selected; they were obviously not picked up off the street, but bought from breeders, but how the masters were selected remained a mystery. Of one thing, however, Ruslan was certain: with a face like his, Master had no need to waste so many words on the Shabby Man, and the latter should long since have been made to stand at attention with his hands down the sides of his pants and sent off to work.

The Shabby Man spoke again: "Where are you headed for, Sergeant? Going to the city or back to your village?"

"Home," Ruslan's master answered reflectively. "What's good about the city? And I need a rest."

"That's understandable. But what about work? I'll bet you've forgotten how to hold a pitchfork."

"Don't need to. I've learned another sort of pitchfork—one with a magazine and seventy-two rounds. Remember, I've been in the service twice as long as you've spent in prison, so I'm due for a pension—the same as they pay a transpolar airman who's flown a million kilometers."

"That's fine, but money isn't a cure-all. If I were you, I'd have waited till now and given myself some nice little wound. Helps a lot, you know; then they give you a disability pension as well."

Master gave him a hard stare.

"I thought we'd agreed not to go on talking like that. You sit here and drink with me, yet you still give me all that crap. It's called 'lack of proper respect.'"

"What—me? Not show you proper respect?" laughed the Shabby Man. "After all these years spent learning it? Don't get riled—you'll sort yourself out soon enough. You're young; life's still in front of you."

So saying, he did something that might have cost him his life: he leaned across the table and patted Ruslan's master on the shoulder. Ruslan sprang to his feet and lunged headlong at the Shabby Man, moving almost soundlessly except for the scraping of his claws across the floor.

Swinging around in a flash, Master stopped Ruslan just in time with a punch of his clenched fist. Though aimed at his jaw, the blow struck Ruslan on the nose and almost sent him rolling away with a howl of pain; but he stood his ground in silence, lest the Enemy see how much it hurt him, and instead only growled at the Shabby Man, whom he could hardly see for tears.

"My God," said Master in amazement, "so it's you, is it, you brute? Scrounging food in restaurants already?"

Still growling, Ruslan rubbed his nose on Master's knee and felt a little better, but when Master stroked him the pain went altogether.

"Does he always act like that?" asked the Shabby Man, who had not even had time to be frightened.

"Like what? Is he always so touchy, d'you mean? Yes, he and I stand up for each other. Don't we, Ruslan? That was how we used to go for anybody if they tried any funny business." Everyone in the restaurant was looking at Ruslan, as though expecting him to do some trick, or perhaps because he was still handsome enough for people simply to admire him, as they had in the past when his master had been so proud of him. Unfortunately, the barmaid was not so pleased with him:

"Citizen," she announced to Master from a dim, smoke-filled corner of the restaurant, "you should take your dog somewhere else. This isn't the camp, you know. It's a restaurant. He's supposed to wear a muzzle in public places."

"What for?" Master smiled at her. "He's never worn one in his life and he's managed O.K. without it. You can have him yourself, if you like.... Why shrug your shoulders?

He'll earn his feed—he won't let the public health inspector through the door!"

"The inspector doesn't worry me. But I've given you an official warning. If that dog bites anyone, you'll have to pay a fine. Plus the cost of antirabies shots."

"Hear that, Ruslan? Take note. You're running around without a license."

Ruslan twitched his ears slightly, creased his forehead into a look of suffering and shifted from paw to paw. If people were expecting a trick, they were virtually seeing one now, so eloquent and clear was the message that Ruslan was able to express: that he found it strange for people to be talking such nonsense about him, that he was embarrassed by this stupid woman who was being nasty to his master on his, Ruslan's, account and that he wanted to get out of here as quickly as possible but was waiting until his master was ready.

Leaning back in his chair, Master gave a belch of repletion and took out his cigarette case. He could feel hostile looks directed at him and was slightly unsure of himself; on such occasions the lighting of a cigarette turned into a complete ritual: he spent a long time selecting a cigarette, tapped it on the lid with its engraved picture, blew into it with a whistling sound and then, scrunching the cardboard mouthpiece, rolled it around his mouth in a spiral. Biting the mouthpiece greedily with his small, even teeth, he squinted down at the tip as he lit it, drew in a lungful of smoke and then blew out a smoke ring while he held the cigarette between the extended fingers of his outstretched hand.

"He's a problem, you see," he said to the Shabby Man, nodding toward Ruslan. "Nobody would take him even if you paid them. And now these fine dogs are just running around on the loose."

"Yes, say what you like, it's a pity," the Shabby Man replied. "When we were behind the wire we used to wish all those beasts dead, yet now I feel sorry for them. It would be better if they'd all been put down, instead of leaving them like this."

"That's just the trouble. Everyone's full of pity, I notice, but as for shooting the dogs—no thank you, someone else can do that."

"I suppose *someone* was ordered to do it?"

"So what if they were? The man who gave the order has already put his epaulets in mothballs and by now he's trying on his civilian suit. Why should I dirty my hands? Not me, if I can help it. But you can see what pity does, can't you? The end result's the worst of all."

As Ruslan understood, his master was still feeling upset at that stupid woman, and he pushed his nose into Master's hand, resting on his knee, The hand was raised reluctantly and placed on Ruslan's forehead. Although neither very fond of a show of affection nor accustomed to receiving it, he still appreciated this gesture on the rare occasions when it was made. This time, however, Ruslan did not like the feel of Master's hand. It was limp, indecisive and for some reason it was trembling; worse still, it stank of the filth in the decanter.

"Don't worry, Ruslan old boy, you'll find your feet," said Master. "And when the call comes, you can go back to the Service. Haven't forgotten about the Service, have you? Still dream about it at night? Ah, yellow eyes! Shut your eyes, they're terrible to look at."

Slowly the hand slid across Ruslan's closed eyes, and as it passed over his jaw it was suddenly closed in a harsh grip. Forced together with a loud snap, Ruslan's teeth pinched his lips, and the pain caused tears to spurt up beneath his eyelids. Worse than the pain, though, was the feeling of resentment. One of the masters' more unpleasant habits was to make a sudden grab with the hand; if they were doing it to a dog, they would snatch at the muzzle—if to a man, they went for his face. When they said it in words, the gesture meant, "Talk to me like that and I'll bash you into pulp." The action itself, though, was much quicker; neither dog nor man ever had time to step back or dodge. And it was a long time before they recovered. One day his master had done it to a prisoner who had been arguing with him and would not step back into line. Afterward the prisoner simply stood there as though stunned, with a pale, sweating face. His glasses had fallen from his nose. The man was very fond of his glasses, because he would frequently breathe on them and wipe them with a cloth; now he did not even bend down, although Master reminded him, "Pick up your specs!" and kicked them toward him with the toe of his boot. So *this* was what that prisoner had felt on his face when he had stumbled back into the ranks like a blind man, and then screamed and started running across the field— the same prisoner whom the unfortunate Rex had failed to catch!

"Don't squeeze him like that," said the Shabby Man. "That devil will bite you if you don't look out—and I wouldn't blame him!"

"Shows how much you know about him," Master grinned, "Ruslan and I have been welded together by the Service, haven't we, Ruslan?"

Freeing himself from the detested grip, with a painful turn of the head and a sullen glare from under his high forehead, Ruslan slowly looked around at the other people sitting in the restaurant and raised unblinking eyes to his master. There was still some uneaten food on the table, but from youth Ruslan had been strictly taught not to beg, and he did not even look at the food. His glum stare, in fact, was not asking for anything, but only a fool or a blind man could have failed to read what it was saying: "You're being unkind, Master. That was a bad joke. And in front of strangers, too."

The Shabby Man suddenly frowned, grabbed a slice of bread from the table and put it on the floor. Ruslan neither noticed it nor looked down.

"Aha, so you thought he'd take it!" Master smirked in great satisfaction. "Of course, he's been dreaming all his life of eating a piece of bread from your hands."

"O.K., you're the boss. Give it to him yourself."

The other customers in the restaurant were no doubt expecting to see Ruslan perform a simple but always successful trick. Our hearts are invariably touched when our four-footed friend displays the rudiments of reason and does violence to his own nature by refusing food from a stranger and then immediately grabbing it, drooling with hunger, from the hand of his master. This time, however, the trick turned out to be even more entertaining than anyone expected: the bread did not leave the Master's hand, and Ruslan merely looked at it and backed away—carefully, so as not to overturn the slice of bread by mistake.

"Aha!" the Shabby Man was triumphant. "That shows that you mean nothing to him now, don't you see?"

"What's the matter with you, Ruslan? Fussy?" Master asked. A pink flush spread slowly over his face. "Suppose you found enough to eat somewhere else. Don't waste much time, do you? All right then"—he put the slice of bread on the floor—"pick it up. D'you hear me?"

"Stop throwing food around, Citizen." The barmaid intervened again. "As if I didn't have enough to do, without having to clear up after your dogs!"

"Why? He'll take it, Just you watch."

Still grinning, though his cheekbones were turning pale, Master picked up the bread and jauntily waved his fork in the air. He dug the fork into a pot on the table and began thickly spreading mustard on the slice of bread.

"Don't do it," the Shabby Man begged him.

A man standing in line at the counter also spoke up:

"Don't play the fool, Sergeant."

"Impossible," Master explained. "It's impossible for him to disobey my order. Don't worry, he knows he's committed an offense by not obeying the first time. So he's got to take the consequences. This dog's loyal to the Service; he'll show you right now just how loyal he is.... Afraid I've used up all your mustard, ma'am!" Master grinned cheerfully at the barmaid.

He broke the slice of bread into two and put the halves together with the mustard inside.

"Feed, Ruslan, feed. Take it, I say!"

A man in a leather coat, sitting with his back to Master, turned around, the whites of his squinting eyes ablaze:

"Have you gone crazy, by any chance?"

"I'll give you 'crazy' in a moment," said Master. "Mind your own damn business!"

The leather-clad man did not, however, turn away. The woman sitting with him, who was wearing a gray headscarf and feeding a child with a spoon, put down the spoon and covered the child's eyes with her palm.

"Keep out of it, Tolya," she begged. "You know better than to get mixed up with them. We won't look."

But she did look, frowning and biting her lip. The whole restaurant was now watching and muttering:

"Don't be cruel to the dog, soldier!"

"Monsters—they learned that sort of thing in the prison camps...."

"He's drunk, can't you see?"

"Why doesn't somebody take the dog away?..."

"Take the dog away? He'd tear you to pieces if you tried to..."

Held in his master's hand, the piece of bread swayed in front of Ruslan.

"Come on, take it! You know you've got to take it!"

What did Ruslan know about that smell? He knew what a guard dog should know, because it was the very stuff that was used to teach them their first lesson. One morning, when he was still little more than a puppy, Ruslan had been taken out into the exercise yard before being fed and his master had left him, saying, "You can run around a bit, Ruslan." Immediately the strangest thing happened. As though materializing from the ground, a Stranger appeared, wearing a padded jacket under gray overalls. Something was hidden in his long sleeve, and he showed it to Ruslan, holding it right under his nose. It smelled so delicious that his mouth watered. Ah, but nothing was quite so simple as it seemed! His clothes gave off the strange smell of those huts in which, as the dog already knew, "bad people" lived, a smell that had already caused him to utter an automatic "Grr-r-r-r!" But the sun was delightfully warm, his mind was still blunted by morning lassitude and by a comfortable certainty that everything in life was for the best. And so poor is our abundant world that every living creature values food and will fight for it, even when still blind and sucking at his mother's nipples. The man presumably valued the food, too, since he did not throw it on the ground but offered it on the palm of his hand, with a smile, like a priceless gift. With an answering smile of the eye and a wag of the tail, Ruslan took the piece of food in his teeth. While held in the teeth it tasted even more delicious; the savory scent tickled his palate and made such a gorgeous pricking sensation on the tongue that it was impossible not to bite into it. So the dog chewed, still wagging his tail and with still-dry eyes thanking the Stranger, who had started to walk unobtrusively away. Next moment Ruslan thought his mouth was on fire, as if someone had thrust a lump of burning tow into it that simply would not go away, that no amount of painful retching and coughing could remove, that was burning his innards and making him see a pall of smoke in front of his eyes. He heard the man laughing as he ran away and felt a furious surge of resentment. Hatred overcame the pain and drove him to pursuit; the man seemed in no hurry to escape, but held out his long, thick sleeve for Ruslan to sink his teeth into.... Finally the unsuspecting Master returned; at last there was someone to whom he could complain, who would understand everything and take pity on him, who let him drink his fill and fed him with special delicacies. Would it all be forgotten? It probably would have been forgotten if those nasty prisoners had not constantly thought up new tricks to play, each one more cunning than the last. But none of their dirty tricks was as shocking as the first one, which had caused Ruslan to make his first little step toward the truth—namely, that absolutely anything that did not come from Master's hand was filthy, poisoned, tainted and sinful, even if it smelled delicious.

Now he was being made to take poison from Master's hand, too. And he knew he would have to take it. He had seen his master's face in every kind of mood, but he had never before seen it looking pitiable as it was now. The joke had gone on too long and Master would have been glad to have put an end to it, but this was exactly what all these strangers wanted and Rush could never obey *them* on any account. If this had been happening somewhere else, Ruslan would have disobeyed; he knew his rights, and he had a way of insisting on them with a low but menacing growl, mouth shut and eyes half closed, while turning himself into a block of stone that would yield neither to threats nor blows. In front of strangers, though, he would never do this, and however stupid the joke might be, Ruslan was obliged to go through with it. Reluctantly opening his teeth, he took the bread, while glancing around for a suitable place where he could take it and drop it.

Master took Ruslan's jaws in both hands and clamped them forcibly together. Ruslan jerked backward, but the hands held him fast, and soon he felt a burning pain in his gums. He tried to unclench his jaws and push out the poison with his tongue, which only made it worse as the fire enveloped his tongue and palate and even seemed to penetrate his ears with a ringing noise. Everything—the dimly lit restaurant wreathed in blue tobacco smoke, his master's pink face—grew blurred in a flood of stinging tears. In order not to prolong the torture he started to swallow convulsively, but the fire only broke out more violently in his stomach, which was already tender from the nausea brought on by hunger. Frightened to death, reduced instantly to sick helplessness, the thought of biting those hands did not even occur to Ruslan; instead he simply staggered backward in an attempt to get away from them, his claws slipping on the floor, with a single idea in his mind—the same idea that had possessed his ancestors whenever wounds or illness had made them suffer: to escape, to crawl away to some dark lair or corner, into the forest undergrowth, into reeds or dense grass, and there to endure his agony alone until he either recovered or died.

Eventually another pair of hands seized him by the collar and dragged him away from Master's grip. Ruslan now moved purely instinctively toward the source of the light and the frosty air, which he gulped hungrily with all the power of his lungs, gasping for breath as he was wracked by a violent, exhausting spasm of hiccups.

"O.K., Ruslan, let's make up and be friends," he heard Master say with unusual affection but in a voice apparently muffled in wadding. "Where are you going? Come here!" With a shudder Ruslan turned and glanced all around the restaurant with streaming eyes. The faces swam, shimmered and went double. Among them he was just able to recognize Master's face—no, there were two Masters there at once, both smiling guiltily, both pink with lackluster eyes. Both faces gave an order in the same voice, saying, "Heel, Ruslan!" And he tried hard to decide which of the two he was supposed to obey. Which of them was his erstwhile, beloved master, and which was the traitor whom he should attack? Unable to solve this dilemma, he decided to leave them both.

Even before he was out of the doorway he heard the people start angrily shouting at Master, who replied in a voice that ended in a shriek: "You mind your own business—I know what I'm doing! It was time to wean him away from the Service. Everyone says they pity the animal—but no one has enough pity to kill him!" Ruslan stopped and thought for a moment: those people might attack Master, and he didn't have his gun. But the suspicion Ruslan had harbored on that first snowy morning, that Master no longer needed either his gun or his dog, had now only been confirmed in bitter and humiliating fashion. Master knew best how to live his life from now on; let him fend for himself. In any case, no one in the restaurant was attacking him.

Head lowered, Ruslan again crossed the main station hallway, cautiously went down the steps and moved along the frostbound wall of the building, trying to keep as close to it as possible. Turning the corner, he took a mouthful of snow. The cold made his gums ache, but it also began to quench the burning sensation. He regurgitated a lump of frozen snow mixed with bread and clots of mustard and noisily retched up the rest of the fiery poison. Still tormented by hiccups, however, and feeling very sick, he looked for somewhere to hide. The pathway led to the same garbage cans where the hunger-maddened Thunder had met his end, behind which was the yellowish-white wooden shed housing the toilet, and there, in the narrow gap between them, he lay down and rested his head on his forepaws. The stench did not bother him, because he could no longer smell anything, and he welcomed the comforting warmth given out by the toilet and the garbage cans. Soon Ruslan felt pleasantly warm; he ceased to toss and turn, and only his eyebrows twitched occasionally at the sound of a voice, the crunch of footsteps in the snow or a locomotive whistle.

His master no longer loved him. This is always a shattering discovery for a dog, filling his whole being with misery and taking away his will to live. It shattered Ruslan, too, even though it might seem that he had grounds enough to guess at it earlier. Perhaps he had indeed guessed it already, but it had somehow been easier to eat a whole jar of mustard rather than acknowledge that he no longer loved Master. For what was it, if not love, that had enabled him to endure the intolerable life of the Service? What was it that had helped them, a fearless handful of masters and dogs, to hold down the thousands-strong herd of prisoners when, had they only combined and mutinied all at once, no amount of machine guns and barbed wire could have kept them under control? What was it that had flung Ruslan into the thrilling pursuit of an escaping convict, into the dangers of close combat? Was not his sole reward to please his master? And was it only because he fed him that Ruslan forgave the Corporal for all those undeserved kicks and shouts? Everything unpleasant that had happened in those days had happened between "us"; no strangers from the world of "them" were ever allowed to witness the humiliations of the Service. Therefore to belittle Ruslan in public could only have been done by someone who did not love him, someone who had betrayed everything that bound them together, who had even betrayed the Service itself, which could not have existed without love. Those hands had made him take something that he was trained to expect only from an enemy; therefore his former master had become an enemy. Master could live the rest of his life as he thought fit; but how was Ruslan to go on living?

One thought occurred to Ruslan: a dog sometimes changed masters. Thunder had had three of them and it did not seem to matter; twice he had grown accustomed to a new master and had loved them both almost as much as the first one, whom he had been given at birth. Other dogs, too, had adapted to new masters, although the results had not always been entirely happy. But above and beyond it all there was the Service. Masters might come and go, but the Service went on forever, for as long as there existed that world surrounded by double rows of barbed wire with watchtowers at the corners, bathed in the glare of floodlights, echoing to the sound of music and voices from black bell-mouthed horns that seemed to dangle from the sky on invisible wires. Ruslan did not know when that world had begun—and he could not imagine it ending. But there must be an end to this terrible stage of homelessness, and he did not care how that end came; amid the mass of small gray details that made up his present existence, Ruslan was kept going by a dream and could already envisage its final glorious outcome: one day the door of his kennel would be open and "Comr'd Cap'n P'mission Tspeak" would bring him a new master—wearing squeaky new boots, carrying a feeding bowl full of delicious-smelling broth and marrowbones; he would put his offering on the floor and say in an unfamiliar but godlike voice, "O.K., Ruslan, let's get to know each other," and Ruslan, wagging his tail, would start eating the food—in token of his absolute trust....

The sound of someone's hesitant, searching footsteps disturbed his thoughts. He noticed that the twilight had deepened, and decided not to go out but to stay hidden, screwing up his eyes in order to be completely invisible. But that someone, whoever it might be, had apparently spotted him, because he stopped and took a timid step toward Ruslan.

"So there you are," said the Shabby Man in astonishment. "What are you doing among all these nasty smells? Lost your nose? Or have you come here to die, Ruslan?" He took another step forward and cautiously squatted down on his haunches. "God, was he cruel to you, that monster! You can never trust a screw. They're all born godless bastards and godless they'll die, with nasty little plywood pyramids over their graves and never a cross. Come on, get up, old boy—no sense in lying here. He's gone now, your beloved master.

Gone away—whoo-whoo—and won't come back. Why don't you come along with me, eh?"

The words flowed toward Ruslan, poured into his keen ears and suspicious heart, and from their general tenor he gathered the fact, floating like a chip of wood on a bubbling stream, that his master was gone forever. Ruslan took this news calmly, even with indifference; having come down from the firmament of his dream to the dirty, stinking earth, he found to his amazement that he now felt a far greater interest in the person who was squatting in front of him. To Ruslan his master was now dead, and this man, his beetling brows topped by a dirty cap with dangling earflaps, was alive and was inviting Ruslan to go with him. For a start, Ruslan would have liked to sniff that cap and the frayed sleeve of his patched overcoat.

Just then the Shabby Man, as though responding to Ruslan's wish, stretched out his hand toward him—slowly, and ready at any second to pull it back again. He did not know that he would never manage to do it quickly enough; nor did he know that the only way to stroke Ruslan was to spread all the fingers open wide to show him that the hand was harmless, and for a start the hand was pushed away by a blow from the dog's bony muzzle. The Shabby Man did not risk a second attempt. Suddenly Ruslan himself stretched out toward him. Rising up on his forelegs, he slowly and deliberately sniffed at the man's cold knee, then caught his wrist, held it gently in his teeth while for several long (and to the man, agonizing) moments he inhaled the warmth and the smell of the coat sleeve. He wanted to make sure that he had not been mistaken, when earlier, in the restaurant, that hand had put food in front of him.

No, he had not been mistaken. The Shabby Man's clothes

might rot away and he might change them for others, but he could not change his skin, and until the skin itself perished it would probably secrete in its pores that impenetrable, irremovable smell—the smell of clothes baked in a prison delousing chamber, of underwear soaked a hundred times in the copious sweat of fear and weakness; the smell of illness and of medicines that never cured them because they all had the same name—"hopeless expectation"; the smell of a bonfire, at which the man had stared with dilated pupils as he tried to keep alive a sudden upsurge of hope, and the smell of that hope as it faded away in flabby muscles; the smell of wooden bunks, hard, but that gave sleep as deep as death; the smell of terror, of longing, of yet more hopes, and the smell of tears that the man had sobbed into his mattress, pretending he was coughing.

Having breathed in this bouquet, Ruslan stood up and allowed the Shabby Man to stand up, and they set off side by side to where the Shabby Man wanted to go—both comforted that they had found each other. The Shabby Man, no doubt, was thinking how easily, by what a lucky chance he had acquired this handsome dog, strong and naturally loyal, who needed no training and who from henceforth would be his companion and defender.

As for Ruslan, this new acquaintance had a different meaning. Although not foreseen by the regulations of the Service, what had happened by no means ran counter to its principal rule: an inmate of the camp had himself asked a guard dog to act as his escort. Although he had been released, the man obviously wanted to return to the shelter of the old, familiar abode. There was nothing surprising in this; it had happened before that runaways had voluntarily returned, half dead with hunger and scarcely able to stand, after spending a whole summer wandering in the forest. When these men came back to camp, the masters generally refrained from beating them up and did not set the dogs on them, but merely gave them a long, cold, mocking stare until, as often as not, the wretch collapsed as though dead at their feet.

The Shabby Man was clearly on the way to going back, and Ruslan regarded it as his duty to guard him until the masters should return. When they did come back, they would replace the overturned fence poles and the torn barbed wire; the black-ribbed machine-gun barrels would be put back in the watchtowers, the red banner with its mysterious white markings would blaze across the gateway in the glare of searchlight beams again ... and then the Shabby Man would go where Ruslan wanted him to go.

3

AT THE VERY START OF HIS NEW SPELL OF DUTY, Ruslan discovered that his prisoner had managed to acquire a master, for the first thing the Shabby Man had to do when he walked into the yard was to ask permission from him (or rather from *her*, since this master wore a skirt and a fluffy headscarf) to bring Ruslan home with him:

"Hey, Stiura, where are you?... Look at the fine guard that I've brought you. You won't chase us out, will you?"

Stiura, a large and portly lady who shut out almost all the light when she stood in the doorway, inspected Ruslan from the porch and was not pleased.

"I'm not sure whether you brought the dog or he brought you. And what are we supposed to feed the brute on?"

"That's the good thing about him—on nothing. He doesn't need feeding. He's funny that way, but he won't be any trouble to you."

The last remark completely reassured Stiura.

"O.K., he can live here—provided he doesn't gobble up my little Treasure."

Ruslan did not wait to be invited indoors. Squeezing past the landlady, he went through to the living room and soon returned. Stiura owned one half of the house, and Ruslan had to check that the windows of her two rooms and kitchen gave onto the fenced yard, so that there was no way for his prisoner to slip out of the house unnoticed. There was one thing, however, that Ruslan was surprised to find—obvious traces of the quite recent presence of the Chief Master, "Comr'd Cap'n P'mission Tspeak." This familiar scent reassured him; besides which, the fact that the boss had personally visited and inspected this place relieved Ruslan, as his subordinate, of any responsibility,

Despite the assurances that he needed no feeding, Stiura nevertheless offered food to her new lodger—a bowlful of hot soup with bones in it. There followed several agonizing minutes in which Ruslan almost fainted with temptation and which consequently rather spoiled this little ceremony of induction. The bowl had to be removed untouched, at which the Shabby Man was triumphant and Stiura was offended, promising that she would send him to the knacker's yard the very next day:

"And there," she said, "they'll make a lo-ot of soap out of you! You'll see."

Sustained by only the shakiest of hope, Ruslan went to sleep on the porch, feeling irritated and savagely hungry. More than once he was wakened during the night by a drowsy cackling that came from the hen coop, and each time he went and inspected it to make sure that the door on the hen coop was tightly shut and the bolt could not be pushed back with his paw. On each occasion he could hear, coming from under the house, a faint growl from the invisible Treasure, who had not yet dared to emerge and make his acquaintance.

Toward dawn Ruslan felt very bad, and he began to have the most grotesque dreams about mouse-hunting: mice the size of cats were actually leaping out of the snow, forming up into ranks of five and marching, with squeaks of joy, into his open mouth. He growled and woke up.

The Shabby Man was not yet up and about, so Ruslan decided to make a brief trip to the forest. On his return, he ran around the entire block, in case the Shabby Man had slipped out by some escape hole or had climbed over a fence. It turned out, however, that he had not yet even come out onto the porch, although the sky had already turned pink and everything in the yard was glowing in bright colors. Then Ruslan remembered that yesterday evening his prisoner and Stiura had together drunk a great deal of that nasty clear liquid before collapsing, apparently dead. Before that he had talked very loudly with a stupid look on his face, waved his arms aimlessly and burst into song—in short, he stopped understanding what was what, just as dogs did. With dogs, however, this sad state came about by itself as a result of old age, whereas humans actually made a positive effort to induce it. This observation struck Ruslan as both interesting and hopeful: however much he might despise that disgusting liquid, it at least gave him the chance to go hunting. He even had time for another nice long sleep before his prisoner finally condescended to emerge—badtempered, with a puffy face, and exuding an even more revolting smell than on the previous evening. God's good daylight did not please him at all; he pulled a face as he looked up at the sky, then spat and made off unsteadily for the little wooden shed in the yard.

At that moment Treasure appeared from beneath the house. He stretched, yawned pleasurably and then, in the middle of his yawn, wagged his little stump of a tail in greeting, as though seeing Ruslan for the first time. He turned out to be a totally insignificant dog, in appearance quite out of keeping with two rumbling *R*s in his name: squat, bandy-legged, with a distended stomach, permanently drooping ears and a coat dotted with random blobs of black, white and tawny red. Ruslan scarcely deigned to glance at him. By making his appearance so late in the morning, when the new canine lodger had already investigated the yard, Treasure thereby waived his own right to the territory, tacitly admitting that he was the junior. Ruslan, however, had no wish to lay any claim to the territory; all his behavior made it clear that he was only interested in the man who was hiding in the shed—and Treasure fully understood this. With a sidelong glance at the door of the little shed, he pulled a face with a very complicated set of meanings: it conveyed sympathy for Ruslan, together with utter scorn for the Shabby Man; it also described his own unappreciated qualities without false modesty, and included the eternal complaint, "What a life we lead, eh, neighbor?" If the Shabby Man had been a master instead of a prisoner, Treasure would undoubtedly have been made to pay for such a subversive remark, but now Ruslan simply turned away, not wishing to get drawn into conversation.

The Shabby Man spent a long time in the shed, grunting, groaning and snorting, obviously undecided about what to do and how to start the day; finally he came out and uttered his first articulate words:

"Where the hell did I put that canvas mitten? One of them's here, but I seem to have dropped the other one somewhere. I suppose you haven't seen it, have you, Ruslan?"

Ruslan merely looked at him with cold amazement. He was being asked to find something, and although he knew where it was, there was no question of his carrying out an order given by a prisoner. Using his own language, Ruslan reminded the prisoner of this fact by getting up, but merely in order to move a short distance and lie down again.

Watching this scene with the keenest interest, Treasure dived headlong under the porch and dragged out the missing mitten. He did not, however, take it to the Shabby Man, but put it down close to Ruslan, so that Ruslan could have the chance to make himself useful. Ruslan did not even turn his head. The Shabby Man was finally obliged to walk over and bend down, wheezing, to pick up his mitten.

"O.K.," said the Shabby Man, "I'm not proud. But one of us seems a bit stupid. That's the trouble with these army dogs—all they understand is 'woof, woof, fall in, dismiss.' Even our little Treasure has more sense."

This was too much for Ruslan to bear. He walked out of the yard, bounded over the step of the gateway and lay down in the street. He had to admit that he had thought better of his prisoner. In blaming Ruslan for being dull-witted, the Shabby Man had shown that he did not understand the reason why a guard dog should decline to obey him. And why had Treasure rushed to pick it up, anyway? Since it was he who had been playing with the mitten yesterday and had dropped it under the porch, it was only right that he should run and pick it up.

When the Shabby Man came out onto the street, with an old army belt around his waist and carrying a toolbox, he said, "Come on, soldier, let's go." This was the only order spoken by the Shabby Man that Ruslan would ever obey.

Thus began their journeys to the strange job with which the prisoner occupied his mornings—if they could be called mornings. Man and dog would set off for the station, where they would turn aside to walk down the tracks to some distant sidings that were a cemetery for old, derelict passenger-cars. This, then, was their work area, just as the block was their new camp and Stiura's yard was their accommodation zone. They would climb up into the cars—Ruslan leaping up in one bound, the Shabby Man clambering breathlessly up the steps—and move slowly from one compartment to another. The windows had all been smashed or removed, so that there was always a draft blowing; the floors and lower bunks were covered in several layers of snow, and there was a smell of rot, dust, rust, human excrement and every track and station where these cars had been. The Shabby Man would raise and lower the creaking bunks, wipe them clean with his sleeve and measure them with a rule, and then sigh, saying to Ruslan:

"Well, now, what about this little plank—shall we book it in? It's kind of narrow, but it has quite a decent grain. Might do in a pinch, don't you think?"

Ruslan had no objection, so the Shabby Man set about "booking it in." Because his hands were shaking, it was a long time before the screwdriver would go into the groove on the screw head, and he lacked the strength and determination to unscrew the rusty screw in one go. Midway through the operation he took a long smoke break, trying to figure out how to apply a nail claw and lever out the plank without splintering it. Even when he had extracted a plank whole, the Shabby Man was not always interested in keeping it: after smoothing it with the palm of his hand and squinting along it against the light, sometimes even sniffing it, he might throw it out of the window. Then he would sit down for a long time, sighing gloomily, before starting to look for another one. And all the time he kept talking and talking:

"Say, Ruslan, how come you can never find a good plank of wood in the whole of Russia? And yet we're surrounded by forests. There's lumber piled up all around us; that's the reason why. If there was a bit less, we might take better care of it and not sell it to other people—then we'd have enough for ourselves. Guess I'd better stop saying these naughty things. It's your job to see I don't talk so much nonsense, Ruslan."

Once a sly thought crept into his hazy mind, his watery eyes took on a lively glint and puckered with cunning as he stared into Ruslan's sad yellow eyes.

"Hey, feller, why don't we go over to the old prison-camp logging site? We know the way there, and we might pick up a plank or two of good quality lumber at the sawmill. We cut thousands of planks when we were working there." Then he answered his own question: "No, we'd better not go. I'd start to feel afraid of you at the logging site. You and I are friends here, thick as thieves you might say, but out there you'd remember the old days and you might not even let me smoke. Anyway, why do I waste so much time talking to you like this? It's time to bang the rail, like they did in camp for mealtimes, and we haven't done a damn bit of work yet."

Nobody here banged a rail, but by some instinct he guessed—and after the second day Ruslan began to guess, too—that it was time for them to go home. By now he had collected three or four planks, of which he said, "Not much good, but they'll do," although in Ruslan's opinion they were little different from the rejected planks, except that perhaps they smelled a little less moldy. The Shabby Man tied them together with a piece of string and carried them off under his arm. By this time of day the effect of the colorless liquid had worn off, his breath smelled less unpleasant and he strode away along the railroad ties quite briskly, as a prisoner should when returning from work. The only thing that aroused his escort's displeasure was his idiotic singing.

He always sang the same song, in an awful plaintive whine, which made Ruslan want to whine, too:

> *You're a lucky fellow, comrade, you've nothing but the best,*
> *Your wife, you see, has two legs like a proper woman should,*
> *But as for me, why, my wife has one leg made of flesh*
> *And the other one, dear comrade, is made of fucking wood!...*

In the streets, thank God, he stopped this dreadful caterwauling; if he had done it in front of other people, Ruslan would have died with shame.

The planks were put into a shed. There the Shabby Man, humming to himself, sawed them, planed them, took them out one after another and inspected them in the light, then finally took them indoors—by now much thinner, paler in color and even giving off a pleasant smell. Ruslan escorted him into the house, stretched out in the doorway and lay so quietly that they forgot he was there. From Ruslan's viewpoint, the thing that was being put together in Stiura's room and that took up almost the whole of one wall simply looked like a huge box. The Shabby Man called it a "three-door sideboard-dresser." Seated on a stool, he fitted the new planks up against the ones that were already in position, changed them around this way and that and asked Stiura whether she liked the way it looked "like this!" Stiura was ironing a tablecloth on the table, and answered after a brief glance around, or without looking at all:

"Yes, it's fine. What do you mean 'like this'?"

"You always say everything's 'fine,'" said the Shabby Man indignantly. "All you want is somewhere to put your junk.

Can't you see that this plank is upside down? It looks all wrong."

"How can it be 'upside down'?"

"Can't you tell from the grain that the butt end of the wood is at the top? Whoever saw a tree growing with its butt end upward?"

Stiura glanced at it again, knitting her pale eyebrows as though agreeing with him, but she still made objections:

"O.K., so that's how a tree grows. But a plank—what difference does it make which way up it stands?"

This gave him cause for more indignation:

"I know you can't tell the difference, but the plank can. It remembers the way it grew when it was a tree, so it'll dry up with misery and then the whole panel will warp."

"Well, I suppose you must be right," said Stiura.

Triumphantly he replaced the plank in the right position and showed Stiura how this was now "quite a different kettle of fish," and he babbled on while the plank was shaved down until it fitted, then smeared with glue and held in place with clamps:

"Just you wait, Stiura, till we get to the varnishing—then you'll see whether I'm a cabinetmaker or a fraud. You'll see that I never use a pad, only the palm of my hand. You have to rub in the varnish with your skin; otherwise it'll just be dead. Why, before the war I was the only person in the Pervomaisky District of Moscow who could make a dresser in the old Russian peasant style. Or a bureau with a secret drawer. When I've finished this, I'll make you a bureau with a secret drawer. I was famous, Stiura! Two furniture factories competed for me; each one wanted me to go there and pass on my experience to the young apprentices. I went and had a look, but there wasn't a scrap of handwork for me to do at either of them. Know what they were doing? They used hardly any solid hardwood, just took trashy old planks straight off the circular saw and glued them together. And they used compressed wood-shavings, too. All I was supposed to do was to make a few drawings for them and select plywood for the veneers. No, thank you, not for me. My sort of work's different. My work, if you want to know, was shown at the National Handcrafts Exhibition; they were even going to send it abroad, but then they changed their minds—'cause of politics. Know where they put my dresser? In the council chamber of the District Soviet building, right under Stalin's portrait. There's fame for you!"

The next plank proved even harder to fit, so after trying it first one way and then another, he gave up and took a long smoke. Inhaling greedily, which made his prominent Adam's apple slide up and down his unshaven neck, he squinted at the tip of the faintly crackling cigarette and his face was suddenly warmed by a smile.

"There's only one thing I regret," he said, "and that is that I didn't make Stalin's coffin, the dear old monster."

"Yes," sighed Stiura, slicing bread, "I guess you'd have made a good job of it."

"Uh-huh!" he chuckled enthusiastically. "Just imagine getting an official government order for *that* job! There'd have been at least three colonels—no, three generals—at my disposal to get the materials. 'O.K.,' I'd have told 'em, 'I want an unlimited quantity of mahogany by tomorrow. And the same amount of Honduras cedar. Ye-e-es ... Don't forget the teak, either, eight planks of it, and some rosewood.' And I'd have lined the cover with boxwood.... Or maybe dogwood. No, sandalwood's better; it has a strong scent, so the old bastard could go on sniffing it for all eternity. The smell of sandalwood can make you tipsy—even without a bottle. Just so as you stay asleep, old pal, and don't wake up! The best thing you ever did was sleep. People love you much more now you're asleep."

He stared at some vague point in the distance as though looking right through the wall, and his smile was gradually transformed into a fixed mask covering a face that had turned white with anger:

"You did more terrible things than two Hitlers could have dreamed up. God, the fires that must be waiting for you in the next world. You timed it well, old man, cleared off just in time...."

Pain and nostalgia were in the man's voice, and Ruslan shared the same feelings in his own way: he, too, pined for a bygone life and longed to get back to it. But he had the patience to wait, without whining in that miserable fashion. Stiura didn't like the way the Shabby Man whined either:

"See what your silly mooning does for you! What's the point of all that sort of talk? It's just hot air; you can't bring back the past. We have to go on living somehow!"

"As soon as I've put this dresser together, I'll forget it all, as if I'd cut it out of my mind."

"The dresser can wait. You'd do better to put your own life together. You're just frittering the time away. Or are you trying to burn yourself up on purpose? After years without touching a drop, you've turned into a soak."

"That's because I'm making up for all that lost drinking time, Stiura."

"Well, I wish you'd go and make up for that sort of lost time somewhere else. Think I'd hold on to you? No, I'll even pay the fare for you to go back to Moscow. Maybe you'll come to your senses a bit quicker once you get there."

"But how can I leave my work, Stiura?"

"O.K., I agree—since you've started it, you might as well finish it."

"That's not the point. If I only do *one* piece of work, I need to do it thoroughly and properly. I want to feel that I haven't lost my skill. You tell me to go. But who will be waiting for me when I get there?"

"Like you said—you had a wife and children..."

"Yes, and you can add my nephews and nieces and godchildren too. Just think, though, how many years have gone by. I was drafted in 1940 for the Finnish War, but I missed the bus and didn't get to the front. Should have been demobilized then, but they forgot and made me stay on. Then came the World War, then I was taken prisoner, then prison again when we got home—have I been in a few prison camps in my time! My family were under German occupation, so who knows whether any of them are still alive? Supposing I did go back, and I told them I'd been released under the amnesty—what would it mean to them? A convict's a convict; they'd never understand that I wasn't jailed for anything I did wrong. We were all behind bars for one thing—stupidity. Anyone with a bit more brain would have kept out of it. So if you're born stupid, don't be a burden to your family—go and live somewhere else. Why should they get into trouble on my account? That's one thing. There's another, too: they already think I'm dead. In their hearts they've already said goodbye to me. Once in a transit prison, I remember meeting someone who'd been my neighbor—we used to live on the same street before the war. 'God,' he said to me, 'you're alive! I thought you'd been dead for years.' They lit candles in church for us—how can we go back now? Who'll be glad to see us come back from the dead? It's a sin, after all, to light a candle in church for someone who's still alive!"

"Well, why not go to some other district?" asked Stiura, pulling her shawl around her shoulders. "You don't have to go back to Pervomaisky..."

"But where else would I go, Stiura? Where am I living now, after all? I'm living in 'some other district' already!"

Shaking her head, Stiura went out into the kitchen. His eyes followed her with a blazing look as he swiveled around on his stool. After some rattling of dishes she clambered noisily down into the cellar, returning with a plateful of tomatoes and pickled mushrooms garnished with red-currant leaves, and placed a sweating bottle in the middle of the table. The Shabby Man shivered and turned his watery eyes away, but it was obvious that the bottle was the center of attraction, the chief object in the room.

Ruslan already knew that the horrible stuff in that bottle was nicknamed "vodka" (it also had a longer name: "Filthy-stuff-damn-the-man-who-invented-it"), and he could never make up his mind whether the Shabby Man really liked it or not. In the evenings he yearned for it with all his heart, but by morning it made him feel terrible and he hated it. Many times Ruslan had noticed that humans often did things that they didn't like, and without any compulsion—something that no animal would ever do. It was significant that in Ruslan's hierarchy the highest rank was held by the masters, who always knew what was good and what was bad; next in order were dogs, while prisoners came last of all. Although they were bipeds, they were still not quite people. None of them, for instance, would dare to give orders to a dog, yet their lives were partly controlled by dogs. In any case, how could they give sensible orders when they were all so stupid?

They were obviously stupid because they kept on thinking there was some sort of better life far away from the camp and beyond the forests—a piece of nonsense that would never enter the head of a guard dog. As if to prove their stupidity, they would run away and wander alone for months, perishing with hunger, instead of staying in camp and eating their favorite food—prison gruel, for a bowl of which they were prepared to slit each other's throats. And when they did return, looking abashed, they would still go on thinking up new ways to escape. Poor fools! They were never, never happy, wherever they were.

Here, for instance—had the Shabby Man really found a better life here? Ruslan knew perfectly well what it was that kept him and Stiura together—it was the same thing that went on between himself and his various "brides." True, it wasn't the worst thing in life, yet even so these two were not really happy together living under one roof. Otherwise why were they often so miserable and why did they quarrel so much, sometimes to the point of shouting at each other? Even here the Shabby Man remained a typical prisoner, in that he often did what he didn't want to do and his "bride" acted the same way; therefore Ruslan was convinced that when the time came to separate them and take the Shabby Man away to the only place where he could find peace, then he, Ruslan, would feel neither doubt nor pity.

Seated at table, Stiura invited "my two lodgers" to come and eat, but one of them refused without even glancing at the bowl put down for him, while the other one wanted to go on working a bit longer. Yet his work merely consisted of fitting the remaining planks into position, after which he would put them aside again, sit down and smoke a cigarette, purposely delaying his blissful appointment with the bottle.

A curious change had come over him: for no good reason his features glowed with relaxed good humor, yet at the same time he obviously felt a nervous compulsion to fidget and talk unceasingly:

"Well, Stiura, my dear, I was telling you about the Finnish War ... M'm, yes. Officially, of course, it wasn't a war, but a 'campaign,' or rather, 'the campaign against the White Finns.' Dammit, but Stalin was diabolically clever in his way, the old murderer! It was a stroke of genius to call them 'White Finns.' None of us knew whether they were really the aggressors or not, but 'White Finns'—that was clear: they were 'Whites,' and we hadn't forgotten about the 'Whites' since the days of the civil war, so it all seemed quite natural and we knew who we were fighting against. Yet really they were just Finns, the people of Finland. Well, so we beat them ... But it was a funny sort of victory. We sure were glad as hell when they asked for peace. And they were clever. They realized that even if we Russians were ready to go on dying for a great cause and for the Beloved Father of All Peoples, the Finns preferred to stay alive. Much better to make peace and save lives—and they didn't even lose much territory, either. Then, in the World War they played a clever game, too: their troops advanced just as far as the old frontier and no farther, however much Hitler tried to order them to go on. There are some clever people in this world, and we could learn a lesson or two from those 'White Finns'—I mean from the Finns pure and simple."

"Just listen to the way you talk," said Stiura severely. "You shouldn't have been put in prison, you should have had your tongue cut off—that would have stopped your babbling."

"I wasn't put in prison for talking out of turn, Stiura. I was a spy, they said, because I raised my hands in surrender to the hated enemy. So maybe they should have cut off my hands, but my tongue had nothing to do with it."

"How can you tell which country's people are clever and which aren't?"

"This is how I see it, my dear." Anger and irritation were seething in his voice. "A person who insists that everyone else should live the way he lives isn't clever. And a people that thinks the same way isn't clever either. That people will never be happy, even though they may sing songs from morning till night saying how happy they are."

Biting her lip, Stiura cast a frightened, sidelong glance at Ruslan, who turned his glittering eyes aside and closed them, pretending to be asleep.

"Evil people are never happy," she said. "And why aren't we happy? Do you think it's because we are evil?"

"We have our share of evil, Stiura. They don't call us a 'hard' people for nothing. But that's only half the trouble. Other peoples are hard, yet they manage to live well enough. Take yourself, now: you seem to be a nice, kind person, but just think what happens if some little bit of fluff hoists her skirt up higher than you're used to seeing it or pushes her tits out into the firing position: you'd stop and give her a piece of your mind, wouldn't you? If you had your way, in fact, you'd have her arrested."

"Good Lord, she can walk around naked if she wants to! As long as I don't have to look at her, though."

"But what if she likes doing it?"

"I don't care what she likes. Other people have got to like it too. People aren't fools—they know what's decent and what isn't."

"There you are!" the Shabby Man raised his finger in triumph. "You can learn everything you need to know about politics by listening to you women talk. Ah, Stiura, all that time I spent in the prison camps wasn't wasted. Why, you'd never believe the different sorts of people I met when I was inside. Clever, educated people—any number of 'em. I'd still be a dumb old fool to this day if it hadn't been for them. I remember I shared a 'sleeping car' in a camp for two years with a German comrade—you know, he had the lower bunk and I had the top bunk."

"Yes, I know what a 'sleeping car' is."

"He'd been to all sorts of countries and he told me all about them. Course, he was a Communist through and through, but you can't change the national character, and this is what I noticed about him: he saw that the people in another country maybe didn't live the same way he did, but that they lived in a special way, which was *their* way—they had their own kinds of customs, they painted their houses like this or like that, they had their own fashion of singing songs or celebrating weddings. Now, if one of our guys starts talking about where he's been and what he's seen, the most important things, according to him, are that they've organized a Young Communist movement in one place, or that the revolution's just around the corner, or in some other place things are hopeless—they haven't learned Marxism yet and are only at the stage of trade-union struggle. But what *really* bugs him is not the revolution or the Young Communists—it's that things in these other countries are not exactly like they are back home in Saratov. And if you ask him what else he saw that was interesting, he just looks astonished and yells at you: 'Well, if you don't think that's interesting, what else is there?' See what I mean?"

As she listened, with her cheek propped on her fist and a frown on her big white face, she suddenly burst out:

"Well, will you sit down at table or are you going to talk your head off all night?"

He moved over to the table and reached swiftly for the bottle. Forcing himself not to hurry, he filled Stiura's glass up to the level which she showed with her hand and gave himself nearly a full glass.

"That's rather a lot," she said, "for the first drink."

"It all depends on what you're going to drink to. The first drink is to the Big Amnesty. I waited for my little amnesty, and it came—but the Big One is still to come. That'll be when they open all the gates and say to everybody, 'You may go, people! Go wherever you like—and without an escort.' Well, here's luck, Stiura."

With a violent shudder he leaned back and drained the whole glass in one gulp, then breathed hard at the ceiling, his streaming eyes blinking as though he had been hit on the head. Regaining his breath, he dug his fork into the food on the plate, but immediately dropped the fork and hastened to pour out again. Stiura covered her glass with her hand, but when he said, "Go on!" she took away her hand.

Now no longer impatient, he grew relaxed and cheerful, and a sort of game crept into their talk.

"Stiura! Say, Stiura," he asked, "what sort of a funny name is that? I've never heard it before."

"You'd better marry me," she replied. "You'll find out if you take me to the register office. Then you can have all of me."

"I'd never even get all of you into that dresser, Stiura, you're such a bi-ig girl...."

She snorted, pretending to be offended, but soon she was sitting on his knees and the game continued with the help of their hands.

"And what about that boss of ours, the captain? What's he like as a man—O.K.?"

"He's nothing special, your boss. Ordinary, same as all of them."

"All of them, eh? Been having the whole lot? If you have, you ought to know every man's different. It's you women who are all the same."

"He was no worse than you, anyway."

"Crap. You're lying. No worse than me—is that all? Why, he's an outstanding personality, a man-mountain, an eagle! In other words, a tick. When a tick gets his teeth into you, either you pull him out with a piece of your flesh or he leaves his head stuck in you for a souvenir. I'll bet he scraped you good and proper!"

"Like hell! That's all he did, scrape.... The only stiff thing about him was the collar of his uniform."

"But underneath it he was a noncombatant, eh? Ah, it does me good to hear you say that. That calls for another drink."

Ruslan stood up, pushed open the door with his forehead and went out.

The daylight had only just faded, but Ruslan knew for certain that his prisoner would not be going anywhere until late next morning, and "that filthy stuff" would keep him at home more reliably than any guard. Accustomed to treasuring his limited free time, Ruslan could not get used to having it in abundance. Until the sky turned pink again and the world glowed with color, he could sleep to his heart's content, go hunting, check on what was happening at the station and visit some of his friends. The problem was to survive till morning on a stomach so empty that the wind seemed to be blowing through it and a pool of hot water was splashing against its sides. He knew that in the warmth the pangs of hunger grew infinitely worse, so he purposely cooled his belly with snow, stretched out on the sidewalk in front of the gate. This was his invariable post, and a very convenient one it was. From here he could not only observe the street in both directions but also see the porch through the open wicket gate, which was never shut at night. His favorite moment was when the streetlamp on its rickety pole was turned on and threw a cone of yellow light all around Ruslan's post. This light warmed Ruslan's heart, because it so vividly reminded him of the prison camp and his spells of guard duty with his master, when together they patrolled the No-Go zone or stood sentry outside a storehouse; cold and lonely, they were hemmed in by a malevolent, impenetrable wall of darkness, on one side of which was light, fair dealing and mutual affection, while on the other side lurked an evil world of deception, trickery and violence.

Treasure, too, would come out into the cone of light and lie down a little distance away from Ruslan, though each day he moved a little closer. He had, of course, already told his friends about Ruslan, and on the second evening they came to make his acquaintance. First to come was a skinny dog called Polkan, with a scalded flank and a look of fixed puzzlement on his face, a grizzled little goatee beard, and a habit of always nodding his head as though constantly agreeing with someone. Then came the painfully intelligent-looking Druzhok, with a permanent enigmatic frown as though he knew some great secret, but who was really extremely dim-witted and could never even remember who his parents were; elsewhere he generally answered to the name of Mutt. Another visitor was the elegant and highly strung Bouton, terribly proud of his frilly pants and his bushy, ever-stiff tail.

The introductions were entirely one-sided; Ruslan did not deign to acknowledge them by a single look or movement, towering above them with the indifference of a megalith. Treasure contrived to turn even this to his advantage: he, too, lay there in silence, adopting the same pose as Ruslan, with the same disdainful look on his face. His friends bitterly envied him and departed in baffled perplexity.

Later there came a bevy of bedraggled little bitches—all with silly names like Darling and Blackie, and one without a name at all—who spread out in a semicircle and gazed at Ruslan with adoration. Their shameless looks said quite openly, "Oh, isn't he handsome! So big and such lovely long legs! Well, of course, he's from the military. Other bitches would try and flirt with him, but I wouldn't dream of it for a second...." If they were hoping for a passionate encounter, they had come to the wrong place; it never entered their thick little heads that Ruslan was On Duty, and that where sex was concerned he was accustomed to performing as generations of his ancestors had done: an order would be given, you were led out on a leash and shown with whom to do it. When their presence bored him he simply twitched his blackish-mauve lips and bared his fangs—at which they all vanished as though blown away by the wind and Treasure immediately remembered some urgent business in the yard.

None of his fellow guard dogs came to visit Ruslan, and he avoided other acquaintances, valuing solitude above all. In the hours when he lay and watched the onset of evening, from an old habit acquired in his prison-camp days, he would run over the events of the day in his mind and prepare himself for the morrow. Anxiously he racked his brains to make sure that he still remembered everything he had been taught, that he had not forgotten any of the lessons learned by harsh experience and for which, if they were ever to slip his memory, he might have to pay dearly.

... HE WAS COMING AGAIN, THE STRANGER IN the gray overalls that smelled of a prison hut. He was approaching out of the sun, his long, early-morning shadow creeping insinuatingly toward your paws. Be on guard and don't be afraid of his shadow, but beware of his hands, hidden in his thick sleeve. When the sleeve was rolled back the poison would be there, in the palm of his hand. But there was his palm, right in front of your nose—wide open and empty. He only wanted to stroke you—after all, one couldn't suspect a trick all the time! The warm human hand was laid on your forehead; its touch was affectionate and solicitous, making a pleasant languor spread through your whole being and driving away all suspicion. You lifted your head to respond to that touch with the ultimate sign of trust: taking the hand between your teeth and holding it briefly and gently without hurting the man. Suddenly the laughing face was transformed with a sneer of malice; for a moment astonishment kept you from feeling the pain, because you could not grasp where it had come from—and the hand was snatched away, having plunged a barb into your ear....

You had not seen it, hidden between the fingers. Learn to see it.

Once again, Master had only to go away for a moment or two and straight away you did something stupid. The shame of it! And the pain! Worst of all, you had to admit to your own stupidity, because you found that you couldn't get rid of the thing by yourself—it wouldn't come out if you tried to dislodge it with your paw or shake it out by twitching your ear, and whatever you did only made it worse. Your ear was now positively burning, with a raging pain that was making the daylight fade—this day that had begun so well, that had been so cloudless and blue. But there was Master—ah, he always appeared at the right moment and understood everything. He would never punish you, even when you had undoubtedly deserved it. He would take you away, while you cried so much that you could not make out where you were going, and then he would quickly remove that horrible thing and put a damp piece of lint on the place that hurt. You gave just one final yelp, and it was all over: Master was already tickling you behind that ear and it did not hurt at all. But if you were a clever dog, you would think to yourself: next time try to see whether there was anything hidden in a stranger's hand. Or perhaps it wasn't even worth the trouble of looking? Wouldn't it be better to be like Djulbars and not trust anyone—so that no one could ever fool you again?

It was not surprising that Djulbars, who had bitten his own master, always earned top marks for mistrust. It was not so much that he showed exemplary aggression toward strangers; he simply wanted to devour them whole, overalls and all. It happened several times that he went berserk and forgot the rules—and he alone was forgiven for it. Casting aside all reason, he would whip himself into a state of anger five or ten times greater than necessary, until his coat was practically steaming and the whole exercise yard reeked of dog. One lesson, at least, he had thoroughly acquired: if you tried too hard, you got away with it; if you didn't try hard enough, you were in trouble.

"You should all learn, learn and learn again from him," said the Instructor, embracing Djulbars around the neck, and the young dogs, seated in a semicircle, drooled with envy. "If this dog had only two more whorls of gray matter in his head, he would be priceless!"

Djulbars himself, of course, thought he was priceless. Only one thing worried him: if he never let anyone come near him, he would never get to bite anybody! So one day he worked out a trick: pretending that he had at last been fooled, he allowed a stranger's hand to rest on his forehead. The next moment it was in the grip of his fangs. Such a terrible shriek had never been heard on the training ground. The wretched man crashed to the ground, lashing out at the animal with his legs, while the masters dashed to his rescue; they tried both stroking Djulbars and whipping him with leashes; they threatened to kill him—but to no avail. Djulbars had clearly decided that even if it meant death, he would bite off that hand. Just then for some reason Thunder, who was tied up in a distant corner, got it into his head that the screaming man was not a prisoner but his own master; genuinely furious, Thunder barked out to Djulbars to leave his master alone. Djulbars, however, had a real case of lockjaw, and even if he had wanted to he could not have unfastened his teeth without first calming down. When his spasm eventually subsided and he let go of what had once been a hand, the victim was incapable of getting up and the masters had to carry him away.

Thunder was unfortunately never able to put his suspicion to the test: from that day onward his master disappeared from his life. Once again Djulbars not only got off scot-free but became even more famous. And rightly so, for who could better serve as a model to the younger generation? He was always paired off with the gentler, less aggressive dogs who neither understood why they should chase an escaping prisoner (he had done them no harm) nor what it was about the pursuit that made it so enjoyable. Djulbars put an end to all their doubts; with a hoarse bark that meant "Do as I do!" he would chase and catch the runaway, bring him down and savage the victim with such relish that even the dullest dogs could see the point of the exercise.

It took Ruslan a long time to appreciate this, and so he had to be subjected to a lengthy and patient course of being teased. People twisted his tail while he was eating, trod on his paw, pulled away the feeding bowl from under his nose, and to cap it all, when he was tied up to a chain they would douse him with cold water and run away, hooting with laughter. Especially unpleasant were the exercises to train him not to be afraid of shots or blows. Though born utterly fearless, Ruslan found it hard to bear when men in gray overalls fired a huge pistol straight at his muzzle or thrashed him across the back with a bamboo cane. True, he soon learned that this stupid pistol never harmed him and he also grew to tolerate the cane, but the whole point was that he ought not to tolerate it but should dodge, lunge for the arm, chase the man and worry him—all of which he did reluctantly.

"Bold, but not aggressive. A certain emotional insensitivity," the Instructor said regretfully, and his remarks cut Ruslan to the quick. "You're too offhand in your approach to him. With this dog you have to do it more seriously; otherwise he doesn't believe you're in earnest."

The Instructor himself took the bamboo, pulled a hideous face and swung the cane in a terrifying slash.

"Come on, bite me! Bite me properly!"

But Ruslan no more wanted to bite the Instructor's bare wrist than he wanted to be suffocated with a quilt. He tried to seize him gently, without even scratching him. He liked the Instructor, who made the most favorable impression on all the dogs—his mere presence lightened all the hardships of their training. They all loved his leather jacket, which smelled so deliciously of some animal that they longed to rip it into tatters and carry a piece away as a souvenir. They loved the fact that he was so slim and agile, they loved his red forelock and his sharp features, which could only be seen properly in profile—and in that profile they could discern something doglike. Active and tireless, he was always on the move all over the training ground; he could explain everything so clearly to every dog that the animal immediately understood him—better, in fact, than he understood his own master. When carried away by his work the Instructor would bark and growl, and the dogs thought he did it pretty well; in fact, if he were to practice a little more, they might actually be able to understand *what he was barking about*. Then they would have forgiven him for not having such a thick, hairy coat as they had (which was why he had to wear the bare skin of some other animal), for not having entirely given up human speech, which was so disgustingly crude and inexpressive, and for still preferring to walk on two legs when four legs were so much better.

The Instructor had, however, already made a few attempts in this direction, and with some success. One of his methods fascinated the dogs; the Instructor did not use it often, but when he did, the whole exercise became a pure delight.

"Attention!" the Instructor would order, and all the dogs nearly died with the thrill of anticipation. "I will demonstrate!" Dropping on all fours, he would show them how to dodge the stick or the pistol and how to seize the hand holding the weapon. Admittedly the Instructor sometimes got hit on the head or the teeth with the stick, but he kept up the game. He would merely lift one paw from the ground for a second to feel whether he had been hurt, and then gave the order: "That doesn't count. I will demonstrate it again," after which he would give a short, sharp bark and return to the attack until he had carried out the exercise with complete success.

Sometimes the dogs even used a little cunning: one of them would pretend not to understand, just so that they could enjoy the pleasure of watching the Instructor one more time and hear him say: "Attention! I will demonstrate!" How nimbly he ran along the beam—much better than on two legs! How elegant and lithe he looked as he did it, how attractively his sharp shoulder blades moved beneath his leather jacket, the red hairs bristling on the back of his neck; how neatly he bounded over a ditch or an obstacle or ran up the ladder in a single movement! And when he was really in form he could complete the whole obstacle course without stopping, the only sign of effort being a few drops of perspiration on his brow. At the end of the obstacle course one of the masters would be waiting, ready with his reward, and the Instructor would take the tidbit in his teeth, still on all fours, and devour it with obvious relish. Gulping down their saliva, the dogs were by then straining to imitate him and repeat the whole series of exercises at one go.

They would have followed him to the ends of the earth had he but summoned them. Even Djulbars let him do what he would not even allow his master to do—to give him a gentle cuff around the muzzle or open his mouth and feel his bite. The Instructor even put two fingers between Djulbars's fearful teeth and asked him:

"Come on, old boy, bite. That's right, harder..."

The masters could not believe it; they were sure the Instructor would lose his fingers.

"Never!" he replied to them. "A dog will never bite anyone who truly loves him. Believe me, I'm an old dog-trainer, a hereditary cynologist—if you'll pardon the high-flown expression. Only man is capable of such a perverse act."

Of Djulbars he said:

"He's not really a ravening brute. He has simply been traumatized by the Service."

The Instructor indeed loved the dogs with all his heart, but he was also slightly mistaken in his judgment of each of them. He regarded them all as traumatized, once they had been through such rigorous training. But the dogs themselves thought otherwise about Djulbars. He undoubtedly would have liked to bite the Instructor, too, but he was afraid that if he did the other dogs would tear him into little pieces.

And this is what the Instructor said one day to Ruslan—looking him straight in the eyes and in a quiet, sad voice:

"I understand his case, and I know just what is this dog's misfortune. He thinks that the Service is infallible, that the code of the Service is always right. You mustn't, Ruslan; if you want to survive, understand this: look on the whole business as a game. You're too serious."

The Instructor valued Ruslan very highly, even though he did not display the right amount of aggressiveness; in some things Ruslan could do better than Djulbars, and in one respect he was so gifted that even the Instructor could not explain how it was done. This was known as "picking a suspect out of a crowd," and it was Ruslan's crowning achievement, in which he had no equals.

This work—difficult but skilled, requiring thought and a minimum of noise and fuss—was what Ruslan had liked best of all. Yet he could not recall it now without feelings of guilt and sin—feelings that were as vague as his recollection of the man himself who had been the cause of the whole grim business. On appearance alone, Ruslan could not have picked the man out of a crowd of prisoners, yet he sensed that the masters had somehow singled him out—perhaps by the very fact that they seemed to pay him no attention. Indeed, the lack of attention paid to the man was a little too obvious; this was something that would only be noticed by a dog who had been imperceptibly held back when a certain prisoner chanced to step out of line. One or two tugs on the leash were sufficient to accustom Ruslan to treat these particular prisoners with respect. Then one frosty day, when he and his master were freezing with cold at the logging site and had slipped into the mobile guard hut to warm up, Ruslan was amazed to see this same prisoner. He was sitting there, in a place that was strictly off limits to ordinary prisoners, smoking and talking with—of all people!—the Chief Master himself. "Comr'd Cap'n P'mission Tspeak" seemed dissatisfied about something and was giving the prisoner a sharp reprimand to which the latter replied insistently:

"But, Captain, you must put yourself in my position. Don't you see? Put yourself in my position."

He said this several times, pressing his hand to his chest, and Ruslan decided that it must be the man's name. "Put-yourself-in-my-position" then went out in great anxiety, glancing nervously around, and a day or two later the dogs were all taken to look at him—lying a short distance away from the guard hut with a length of steel hawser twisted around his neck. When the man had been alive, Ruslan had never found him in any way memorable, but the sight of him as he lay dead etched itself into the dog's memory: staring up at the sky with glazed, protruding eyes, a purplish-blue swollen face, one arm twisted behind his back and the other flung out to the side, the rigid fingers of the hand clawing at the snow. This hand, the face, and the snow around the head were thickly strewn with flakes of coarse, homegrown tobacco.

One after another the dogs approached the body but could only turn away, blinking and whining guiltily. When it was Ruslan's turn, he had already worked out why they were unable to pick up any scent. They had started from the dead man's head, first sniffing his horrible pale-purple neck with its twisted furrows caused by the steel noose and its lumps of flayed skin, then sniffing the free ends of the hawser stretched out on either side like an unwound scarf; in doing so the dogs had inhaled nothing but tobacco, after which all their efforts were useless. Ruslan began with the hands. Cautiously approaching the extended hand and backing off in time, he next prodded the stiff body with his muzzle to ask for the dead man to be turned over, then carefully sniffed the other hand, which had been clenched so violently that the nails had dug into the flesh of the palm. Here he saw not only the dark-blue blood from the nails, but also the tiny drops of sweat that had exuded all over the hand before death. They had frozen and grown opaque, like spattered drops of lime, but if they could be slightly thawed out by breathing on them...

Closing his eyes, he exerted all his faculties in an intense effort. The masters were meanwhile devising theories as to who might have done it; each one of them had personal scores to settle with various prisoners and their guesses corresponded closely with those particular antipathies, but they were mainly concerned with guessing at how many men had been involved. Three? Four? In so thinking, they were misleading themselves, because one should always start from one. They had eyes to see, and had noticed the tobacco, which had been sprinkled for the very purpose of attracting attention and neutralizing the dogs' sense of smell; but they did not notice, for instance, some tiny scales of tree bark alongside the steel hawser, which was the first thing that Ruslan had spotted. The masters, in general, speculated too much. Ruslan, on the other hand, did not speculate at all, having neither scores to settle nor theories to propound; instead, he simply saw exactly what had happened—in the way that one sees a hallucination or a lucid, coherent dream—and heard the squeak of snow beneath the victim's boots and the nervous breathing of the murderer lurking in ambush.

In the bluish twilight, "Put-yourself-in-my-position" had come out of the guard hut—the very place where the masters used to give him cigarettes—and as he had walked along this pathway, passing between two fir trees, he had not noticed the looped hawser fastened to one of the trees at a level slightly higher than his head. The other end of this noose was held by the murderer, who had swiftly lowered the heavy steel loop, smooth with frequent use and lubricated with axle grease, onto the shoulders of "Put-yourself-in-my-position," and turned around; with the free end of the hawser now over his shoulder, the murderer gripped it with both hands, laid the whole weight of his body against it and took, at the most, half a step forward. The noose tightened, and the murderer could feel the hawser twitching—that was the victim's hands, trying to unfasten the noose with a sudden access of strength brought on by mortal terror and a violent craving for air. Then summoning up all his strength, all his fear and his deadly hatred for the victim who was taking so long to die, the murderer lashed out backward with his boot at the man's legs and kicked them free from the supporting ground. For a further eternity he stood there, close to exhaustion from the strain of acting as both hangman and gibbet, while "Put-yourself-in-my-position" croaked and twitched behind his back, still grasping hopelessly at the steel rope. Once or twice, though, he happened by chance to clutch at the murderer's reefer jacket with the weak, helpless grasp of hands already damp with the sweat of death, a touch so slight that his murderer did not even feel it. But when later the murderer untied the hawser and dragged the strangled corpse away from the tree, when he sprinkled the tobacco and thought how silently and successfully the job had been done, he did not know that along with some minute threads from the hem of his reefer jacket his whole self was held in that clutching fist and in those droplets of frozen sweat; for that hem had rubbed a thousand times against his face and hands, had often covered his feet as they lay freezing at night under a thin blanket—and it was a stroke of luck for Ruslan that a spasm had twisted the victim's hand behind his back, leaving it underneath the body. The clues were found. Ruslan stepped briskly back and nudged his master's knee with his nose, which meant, "I don't promise anything, but I'll try. Lead me quickly."

The actual identification of the suspect proved to be astonishingly easy. Any one of the other dogs, who had given up at the very beginning, could have carried it out—if they had merely had the effrontery to try. Ruslan did not even get very close to the crowd of prisoners, who had been rounded up and made to stand on the open ground in front of the camp gates. As soon as they saw the line of masters slowly approaching, headed by a dog straining at the leash, the entire mob retreated with a roar—leaving behind a single man in a black reefer jacket. Hunched up, his hands thrust under his armpits, he fell forward on his face, shouting hysterically:

"No, not the dog! I'll tell everything. Only don't let that brute get at me...."

Ruslan did not savage the man, but merely gave a gentle bite on the hem of his jacket—in the place where the murdered man had snatched at it—and wagged his tail to show that the search was over. For this he received an unprecedented reward—from the hands of the Chief Master himself—and from that day onward he was acknowledged the champion at "picking a suspect out of a crowd."

Starting from that day of his triumph, there stretched in Ruslan's memory a broad, straight path cut through the forest, along which Ruslan and his master were escorting the man in the black reefer jacket. The wind was sighing in the tops of the great pine trees, and as their branches touched they let fall armfuls of snow, which scattered like iridescent powder. All was silence and peace, and the man walked the whole way calmly and without hurrying, a spade carried on his shoulder or making zigzags in the snow as he trailed it behind him. Now and again he would whistle a tune.

It was obvious to Ruslan that the man was so overawed by the stillness of the forest that there was no possibility of his making a sudden leap to one side in a dash to escape. Still in silence, they turned aside down a narrow pathway to a clearing that had been blackened and charred by a log fire. In the middle yawned a shallow pit, its brownish-red sides still showing the smooth, semicircular marks made by crowbars and the sharp triangles of a wedge. Here the man spoke for the first time, turning toward Master with an angry white face that bore several tiny little scars on the cheek and forehead. He did not like the pit. When he stepped into it, it only came up to his knees and he was so angry that he spat into it.

"I did it by myself, but I did it for them all," he said to Master. "They might have shown me some respect."

"What do you mean—respect?" asked Master.

"I don't mind about the worms, because the worms get everybody in the end—they'll get you when your time comes—but I don't deserve to be dug up and eaten by the wolves. There was nothing about wolves in my sentence."

Ruslan's master very much wanted to smoke. He took out his cigarette case, then put it back into the pocket of his white sheepskin jerkin. Even more than a smoke, he wanted the business to be over.

"You mean, you want to make a complaint against your own work team?" said Master. "There's nothing to discuss about your sentence."

The man spat again, clambered out of the pit and rammed the spade into the pile of freshly dug earth.

"O.K. But just promise me you'll stamp it down good and hard afterward. I don't have any complaints about anybody—it's just that after knocking off that stool pigeon, I don't deserve to be buried so shallow that the wolves will come and chew me up. Will you take back my jacket to them? They can draw lots for it. I'll take it off now to save you the trouble."

Without replying, Master unslung the submachine gun from his shoulder.

"Why don't you answer?" asked the man. "Don't I have any rights at all—even now?"

It was all taking an agonizingly long time. Ruslan was shivering all over and had to clench his teeth to stop himself from howling. Then something went wrong with his master's gun. Try as he might, he could not push the bolt home, and this man was so hoping that on this one occasion it would jam completely; but Master said: "I'll fix it right away, don't worry"—and he did fix it. He extracted the damaged cartridge, the bolt went home with a click and by mistake the gun fired a single round into the air. It was then that the man embraced Master's boots. He crawled up on all fours and pressed his face against them so hard that when he looked up there were black smears on his forehead and lips. He smiled a pale, ingratiating smile and spoke quite differently from the way he had spoken before the crack of the shot and the blue puff of bitter, acrid powder-smoke. He said that the people back at camp would have heard the shot, they would think the job was done and now Master could let him go; he would crawl away into the forest and live there like a snake or a rat without seeing another human being for the rest of his days—of which he probably hadn't many left to live, anyway—and there would only be one person—Master—whom he would consider his brother; he would always pray for him and remember him with gratitude, he would love him more than his mother and father, more than his wife and the children he had never had. Unable to distinguish the words, Ruslan heard more than words: he heard a passionate promise of love, of ultimate true love, the tears of love, and the pounding of blood in the temples—and he felt with horror that he was being filled with an answering love for this man; he believed in his face, with its deep-set, smoldering eyes, in which there burned the fire of pure, unclouded reason. This man did not crave some other, better life that had never existed, but simply the allotted span that is sufficient to every living being on earth.

"What's the matter with you? You're not a little kid, are you? Can't you hear what crap you're talking?" said Master, attempting to stop the flow. He was standing quite unmoved, in no way afraid that the man might pull him down or grab his submachine gun; he knew how helpless any prisoner was against him and how swiftly Ruslan would spring to his help. If he had but known that Ruslan was in the grip of a kind of paralysis and could not even have moved from the spot! "You may get away for a while, but sooner or later you'll be caught and they'll line both of us together up against a wall. Where could you go? You would eat leaves and lizards for a bit, then after a while you'd have to kill somebody again. That's the truth, isn't it? You're not the first, others have tried it.... So forget it. And get up, don't torture yourself with any more false hopes. Don't worry, I won't hurt you, like some others would. Come on, get up, that's agreed—I'll do it so it won't hurt."

The man stood up and wiped his face hard with his sleeve.

"All right, do your stuff. You wouldn't even let me live a jackal's life. You'll remember that...."

"I know," said Master. "I already know everything you're saying. Haven't you said enough?"

He did not hurt the man, but the whole way back Ruslan could not stop trembling. He whined and tried to pull free from his collar, longing to go back and dig up with his paws the frozen lumps of earth that were pressing down on that white, unmoving face. He had never before behaved so badly and his master was obliged to give him a cruel whipping with the leash. Perhaps it was from that day on that his master stopped loving him.

Those frozen clods remained in Ruslan's mind, weighing it down with fear and a sense of guilt, as if he had betrayed his master and disappointed his hopes; he also felt he had somehow revealed that he, Ruslan, was not truly serving as a guard dog but merely pretending—and a dog who did that was likely to be shot without delay, because at any moment he might let the Service down by doing something wrong or refusing to do what he was told. And even though they escorted many more men into the forest, his master never again trusted Ruslan as completely as before.

In his youth Ruslan had been trained in all the skills for which a dog is born; he went through the course of general obedience-training—simple things like "Sit!" "Lie down!" "Heel!"—had passed his tests brilliantly in tracking, identification and sentry duty, but when he moved on to the highest level of training—escort duty—the Instructor had doubted whether Ruslan would pass his final examination. The test was not taken on the training ground, where there was always someone to correct your mistakes, but on real escort duty, where only one order was ever given: "Guard!" From then on the dog was on his own and had to think for himself. And the object to be guarded was not some storage dump, which would not run away and aroused no feelings in the dog, but it was the most temperamental and valuable of all things—people. The dog must always beware of them and must never feel pity for them; the best attitude to adopt toward them was not so much one of anger as of healthy mistrust. "He'll be O.K.," his master had said. "He'll get used to the work. Ruslan won't make any mistakes." And many dogs did make mistakes; many were dismissed as unsuitable and taken away somewhere in a truck—and then only if they were young and might be retrained for some other form of service. Once a dog had served on escort duty, there was only one way to go if he failed—outside the wire.

INGUS DECEIVED EVERYBODY. HE SEEMED SO capable and learned everything so quickly. He captivated the Instructor at his first appearance on the training ground. The Instructor only had time to say, "All right. We will practice the command 'Heel!'" when Ingus immediately stood up and walked over to him. The Instructor was delighted, but insisted on repeating the exercise from the beginning. Ingus went back to his place and came to heel again on the command.

"Extraordinary!" said the Instructor. "And what about 'Sit'?"

Ingus sat down, even though no one had pressed on his back.

"Stand up."

Ingus stood up. The Instructor squatted down in front of him.

"Give me a paw."

Ingus at once did so.

"Not that one—no one gives their left paw."

Ingus apologized with a wag of the tail and changed paws. From then on he only held out his right paw.

"I don't believe it," said the Instructor. "Such dogs don't exist."

He checked Ingus's record card, to confirm that the animal had not already been through a training course and only knew his name and the command "Place!"

"I thought so," said the Instructor. "He has, of course, a unique pedigree. Amazingly successful breeding. What parents! I remember his sire, Remus—a dog of the rarest intelligence. And his dam Naida, of course—a four-time champion. He was bred by Kamil Ikramov, a great expert, who knew how to choose good parents for a dog. Obviously their son was being prepared for Karatsupa, hence his name.* And still I say, 'I don't believe it.'"

---

*At the famous frontier post of Karatsupa, where five hundred illegal border-crossers were arrested, all the dogs were called Ingus. (Author's note.)

He called all the masters together to admire Ingus's unusual abilities, and asked them if they had seen anything like it before. None of them had ever seen his equal. He asked whether they didn't think a man was hidden beneath this dog's skin. The masters did not think so; whatever skin he might put on, no man could conceal himself from them.

"What do I mean by that question?" said the Instructor. "I mean that if such a dog existed in reality, I would not be working here. I would be touring the world with him, and everyone would be amazed at the success achieved by Soviet dog-training, by our humane, progressive methods. Because dogs like this can only be found in our country!"

Ingus listened attentively with his head cocked to one side, as was natural for a young dog, but his eyes were serious beyond his years. From Ingus's very first day at the training school, people noticed a look of melancholy in those amber eyes.

He grew up, and his fame grew with him. With extraordinary ease he progressed from one phase of training to the next, advancing by leaps and bounds. Lean, elegant and graceful, he flew unerringly along the beam, overcame the barriers and mounted the ladder as though it were child's play, jumped first time through the "burning window" (a steel frame soaked in gasoline and lit), while in tracking he displayed an excellent "nose" both on the ground and in the air. He also acquitted himself well enough in the training for guard duty, although he was somewhat lacking in aggression and seemed embarrassed by the antics of the fools in gray overalls trying to snatch the rag-stuffed sack given to him to guard. Although Ingus fully realized that the sack was a worthless dummy, no one ever managed to distract his attention from it, sneak up unnoticed or crawl through the bushes to attack him from behind. He showed that he could see through all their tricks, and even the men in gray overalls felt uncomfortable at his sad, reproachful gaze.

Djulbars began to be seriously alarmed. The acknowledged champion in aggression and mistrust, his ambition was to be first in everything else, even though his nose was mediocre and in picking out a suspect from a crowd he was completely hopeless: whenever he was led up to a group of prisoners, he grew so violently aggressive that he could not tell one man's scent from another and simply made a grab at the one who was nearest. His attitude was that if a dog could not stand up for himself in a fight, then all his other skills were useless, so he tried to savage any young novice dog who threatened to excel him. Ruslan did not escape being challenged by Djulbars, and he felt the onslaught of that broad chest and that battering ram of a head. Although twice brought to the ground, Ruslan not only refused to let himself be bitten but added yet another scar to Djulbars's muzzle—which Djulbars took in good part, even wagging his tail to encourage the young fighter. Ingus reacted quite differently: he simply turned aside, exposing his thin neck to the attack with a mocking smile to show that he saw no sense in this horseplay. The old ruffian, of course, sank his teeth into Ingus's neck without a second thought and would have drawn blood had he not remembered that he was breaking the first rule of a good fight: "bite, but don't kill"—and stopped in time, before the dogs all went for him at once.

Djulbars, however, was soon appeased: he realized (which the other dogs had noticed already) that Ingus was no threat to him. He was not born to be a champion, despite the ease with which he did everything. He had no real drive, no competitive urge. Instead, his eyes betrayed a certain boredom, an enigmatic sadness, and his mind seemed preoccupied with thoughts that were his alone. Soon they noticed something else about him: while Ingus might faultlessly carry out an order ten times, his master could never be quite sure that he would obey for the eleventh time. However much they might shout at him or beat him, he would sometimes refuse completely, and nobody could understand why this happened or when to expect it. He would suddenly fall into a kind of stupor, in which he saw nothing and heard nothing, and only the Instructor could bring him out of this state.

The Instructor would go up to Ingus and squat down in front of him:

"What's the matter, old fellow?"

Ingus would close his eyes, give a faint shiver and whimper slightly.

"Don't overstrain him," the Instructor said to the masters. "This is a rare case, but it crops up occasionally. He already knew all this in his mother's womb before he was born. Now he is simply bored; he could even die with boredom. Let him take a rest. Off you go, Ingus—take a walk."

Thus Ingus alone was allowed to wander freely about the training ground while all the other dogs trained and trained until they were nearly driven mad. It was not hard to predict the outcome: one day Ingus simply ran away from the training ground—and vanished from the camp altogether.

He was supposed to go over the obstacle course—with his master but without a leash. Together they ran along the beam, bounded over the ditch and the barrier, and dived through the "burning window"; next they were supposed to crawl beneath rows of barbed wire stretched parallel to the ground on pegs—but only Ingus's master crawled under the wire, while Ingus himself raced ahead, leaped over a stone wall and galloped away in long, bounding strides across the parade ground. Not even the camp's perimeter fence stopped him; it was easy enough for a dog to crawl under the wire—but how did he pass through that other invisible, psychological barrier standing ten paces in front of the outer wire and as solid as the pane of glass hit by a bird which tries to fly through a closed window? And what was the matter with the machine gunner, whose orders were to fire at any living creature that violated the No-Go zone?

When the masters finally set off in pursuit of Ingus, he had already crossed the open fields and disappeared into the forest. He might have escaped altogether—he could run faster than all the others and he did not have to drag a master behind him on a leash—but here, too, an inclination to daydream was his downfall. What was he doing in the forest when they found him? He was rolling on his back in the grass, smelling the flowers, watching a bug climb up a stalk and following its flight with longing eyes as though entranced.... He did not even notice when the search party surrounded him with shouting and barking, and the spring clip was fastened to his collar with a click; only when his master began to whip him did Ingus finally come to his senses and look at him—with amazement and pity.

Grave doubts were expressed when the time came for Ingus to be mustered for escort duty. The Instructor did not want to let him go, saying that Ingus's teeth were not yet fully grown and it would be better to leave him in the training school to demonstrate the exercises to the novice dogs. But the Chief Master noticed that Ingus savaged the dummy (known affectionately as "Ivan Ivanovich") quite as well as the other dogs, and as for acting as a demonstrator, the Chief Master pointed out that the Instructor was quite capable of doing this himself—that was what he was paid to do—and no funds were available to feed a supernumerary canine member of the instructing staff. The Chief Master decided that he personally would put Ingus through his tests. Everyone grew nervous, most of all the Instructor, who was very proud of his favorite pupil and wanted him to show up to his best advantage. And something came over Ingus: perhaps because he did not want to disappoint the Instructor or because he was inspired by everyone's attention being concentrated on him. Whatever the reason may have been, his performance was unique and magnificent on that day. He escorted three prisoners at once; two tried to run away in different directions, but he brought both of them to the ground without allowing them even to raise their heads, and he did not let up until help came and all three were handcuffed. For five whole minutes he was master of the situation; the Chief Master himself timed it with his watch and said afterward to the Instructor:

"You were wrong to doubt me. It's time for this dog to be working, not sniffing the flowers."

When Ingus was put on escort duty, however, it became obvious that he did not really want to work. Other dogs had to do his job for him. The column of prisoners went its own way, while Ingus pranced along at a distance as though out for a stroll, ignoring obvious breaches of the regulations. A prisoner might step half a pace out of line, might unclasp his hands from behind his back or exchange a few words with his neighbor in the next rank—and at that very moment something would distract Ingus and he would look away. Yet the masters remembered how Ingus had performed at his final test and how the Chief Master had praised him;

that, presumably, was the reason why Ingus was forgiven for things that would have earned another dog a good whipping with the leash. Only the dogs sensed that he was just phenomenally lucky, and that a real emergency, such as an attempted escape, would mean the end for Ingus.

And so he lived on with his inscrutable dreams or, as the Instructor put it, "the poetry of instinct," always likely to join Rex at any time. Yet he did not die outside the wire but in the camp, by the doorway of a prison hut—where he died as the instigator of a dogs' revolt.

Although it was retentive, Ruslan's memory was also prone to reorder events into its own capricious sequence—which nevertheless had a sort of logic. Everything good and pleasant was relegated backward to the time when he was a puppy; there, in the cool, twilit storehouse of memory he would save up the sweet marrowbones to which he could return for consolation at moments of stress. Everything that was bad, on the other hand, all the hurts and afflictions, he kept close to the forefront of his mind as though surrounding himself with a crop of nettles ready to sting him at any moment with their ever-fresh venom. Thus in Ruslan's private chronology, the day of his triumph in picking the suspect out of a crowd was somehow pushed back almost to the dawn of his life, together with the memory of "Put-yourself-in-my-position," the prisoner who had been strangled by a length of steel hawser; on the other hand, because of its bad associations, he was unable to relate positively to the unfortunate dogs' revolt, which seemed to have happened only yesterday. But when memories of the revolt did come flooding back with all their smells, sounds and colors, "Put-yourself-in-my-position" came back with them—alive again as he came into the warm guardhouse, blowing on his hands, to give the masters some alarming news that caused them instantly to throw away their cigarettes and pick up their submachine guns and dog leashes.

The dogs, too, who had grown drowsy and stupefied by the warmth and the delicious odors given off by the masters' sheepskin coats, leaped to their feet and rushed panting out-of-doors, completely forgetting why they had not been sent out on duty that day. God, how the frost gripped their muzzles with its sharp claws! It pierced their nostrils with red-hot needles, blinded them as it made their eyes water and gave them a dull pain in the forehead, as though they had dived headfirst into a hole in the ice. Ruslan could not remember what became of "Put-yourself-in-my-position" at this point; here his chronology lost sight of the man altogether. Either he had remained in the guardhouse, or perhaps it was he, looking frightened and nervous, who had eased the door open and slipped out to hide in the sentry box; or maybe he had vanished somewhere near the hut, had simply dissolved in the mist, crumbling into icy fragments that were blown away by the blizzard. When they saw the hut itself, the dogs began straining to go into action—whatever sort of work awaited them inside, at least it would be warm!—but the Chief Master, who had led the way, turning around every now and again to rub his red face with his mitten, stopped them all outside the door. Advancing stealthily, he opened the door without letting it creak, and bent forward to listen, raising one earflap of his fur cap.

The entranceway of the hut gave forth a gust of heat and the usual smell, together with a buzzing noise—the same sort of vaguely indignant buzz that arose in the dogs' quarters when the food came late. Behind the thin inner door some large object could be heard bumping about, hitting the walls or the floor with a dull thump, mingled with shouts, groans and rapid, angry muttering. It sounded like one of those brawls that humans were prone to start for no good reason, sparked off by a single word in a bad-tempered argument, which escalated furiously and inexorably into a fight, only to cool down as quickly as they had begun, after which all the people would disperse—though sometimes leaving one person lying on the ground clutching his stomach, doubled up in convulsions, or maybe not moving at all.

The Chief Master pushed open the inner doors, flinging them wide enough for a truck to drive through, and stood in the doorway with a visible cloud of cold air swirling up to his waist.

"Shut that door, you son of a bitch, or I'll smash your head in!" This bestial yell, uttered from the murky depths of the hut, was followed by some heavy object flying through the air and hitting the doorpost right alongside the Chief's ear.

The Chief Master waited calmly until the noise had died down.

"I see," he said, rocking back and forth on his heels, hands clasped behind his back. "I see. So we are discussing the fate of the country again, are we?"

The hut was silent, but someone near the door spoke up eagerly:

"Of course we weren't, Citizen Captain. We wouldn't dare. We were just discussing things that we're allowed to talk about in our free time."

"Aha... But as I was walking past just now, it seemed to me that things were getting a bit heated in here. So I thought perhaps you people ought to be given a little work to do. Otherwise you might get bored."

Again the hut answered back—with the same voice, this time accompanied by a faint chuckle:

"We're always ready to work. With pleasure! Only the damn thermometer is showing minus forty-four."

"Oh, you've had a look, have you? I haven't seen it yet. Funny, but I had the impression it had got a bit warmer."

"Citizen Captain!" The voice was irrepressible, seemingly ready to go on chattering forever. "Why do we respect you so much? It's because you have such a nice sense of humor. Come inside, please, so that I can shut the door."

A vague shadow moved toward the cloud and merged with it, but the Chief pushed the shadow away with his hand.

"Sure, I don't mind jokes. I'll even allow debates—when they're orderly and well-behaved. But if the work suffers, then that's bad."

The buzzing started up again in the semidarkness inside the hut, and another voice—hoarse, redolent with sleepy warmth and reluctance to come out into the cold—asked with glum despondency:

"Will you shoot?"

"What d'you mean—'shoot'?" retorted the Chief in amazement. "Why should I shoot, unless there's a mutiny in camp? There's no mutiny."

"That's right!" The whole hut sighed with relief. "There's no mutiny!"

"You see? So why should I shoot? I'd much better make you a skating rink!"

"What sort of skating rink?"

"The usual sort. Never seen a skating rink? Anyone who has a pair of skates can go skating."

The timid shadow approached again, tried to slip through the doorway and was pushed back by the Chief.

"No, it's not good enough if just one or two of you come out. I want all of you out, together."

Silence fell on the hut for a moment, just long enough for someone to cry out in an urgent, pleading voice:

"Come on, fellers, let's go out. It's our own fault, after all."

Immediately the many-tongued brute inside the hut started banging, rumbling and shrieking again:

"Lie down, you son of a bitch, or I'll kill you!"

"There's a law against it!"

"The law says you can't send us out to work when it's minus forty or below!"

"Everybody lie down...!"

"It's the law!"

They did not see that a fire hose was already being unreeled from the water tower. Leaning against the crowbar stuck through the middle of the reel, two of the masters pushed it until they were just short of the door of the hut, where they dropped it onto the snow. Two more rushed and straightened out the kinks in the hose, seized the gleaming yellow nozzle and ran with it up to the doorway. The Chief Master moved aside with a glum look on his face, sadly let out a cloud of steam from his mouth and waved his mitten as a signal to someone in the distance. From the water tower came a barely audible rustle; the flattened canvas of the hose started to come alive, to fill and grow round, a gurgling, high-pitched hiss came out of the nozzle and the two masters in the entranceway staggered slightly. A thick blue jet struck the ceiling inside the hut, then moved lower down, sweeping away a man lying on an upper bunk, together with all his belongings, and forced back into the hut a number of timid shadows who tried to run forward through the door. The two masters, jamming down their boot heels to keep a foothold in the slippery doorway, could hardly control the heavy nozzle as the jet of water sprayed from side to side, striking blows that were as hard and resonant as the blows of a club. A white cloud poured out of the hut above their heads, and along with the hot, stuffy air there came not a scream, not a shriek but a gasping, long-drawn-out sigh, such as a man gives before a long plunge into the water.

Ruslan's ears were so filled with the sound of that sigh that he hardly heard the windowpanes shatter and the frames crack, and at first he did not realize what the gray, smoking foam was that was crawling out of the windows and onto the snow; he only understood it when the foam began to separate out into men, who struggled to get up while others fell on top of them. The Chief Master raised his hand from behind his back and pointed in their direction, at which the hissing jet was aimed at them in a smoothly curving arc and was held there for a long time before being directed back into the hut. By then the men who had fallen out of the windows no longer attempted to get up but simply twitched feebly as they lay on the snow—and turned white in front of the watching eyes.

Unable to sit still, Ruslan fidgeted and yelped, nervously lifting one paw after the other. As those white spangles encrusted the men's clothing like chain mail, he seemed to feel them on his own coat, thick, furry and warm despite the ice-cold wind blowing through it. Gradually the white spangles started to turn yellow, which happened to Ruslan whenever he got very angry, until the only thing that he could see clearly through the yellow film was the thick hose wriggling in the snow. As this reptile crept toward his paws, it squirted water out of small holes in its side, and in one place, where the masters had been unable to straighten it out, it was twisted into a crease that had risen up and was now swaying right in front of Ruslan's nose, threatening to attack him but always falling back whenever Ruslan made a dart at it.

Luckily for him, there was another dog, younger and rasher, who was the first to lose patience. Ruslan heard a spine-tingling growl, and across the edge of the yellow film there flashed the dog himself—dark gray and slim, body extended in a flying leap. In midair Ingus seized the thing that was threatening Ruslan, sank his teeth into the hose and pressed it down with his paws. The hose immediately began to struggle free, and this infuriated Ingus even more; snarling with frenzy and shaking his head from side to side, he tore at his enemy, water squirting out of his mouth in a rainbow-colored spray. The two masters holding the nozzle shouted and pulled the hose toward them, pulling Ingus with it. At the same time his leash pulled him backward, throttling his slender neck. A haze came over Ingus's bloodshot eyes, but he would not let go of his prey.

"What's the matter with him?" asked the Chief Master. He walked slowly over, a demigod with terrible blue eyes and an angry face, holding up the blue vault of heaven with his fur cap. But Ingus was too preoccupied to give him more than a glance. "What's the matter with him, I say? Has he gone crazy?"

"God knows, Comr'd Cap'n," said Ingus's master. He was in despair. He kicked Ingus in the flank. The dog squealed painfully, but would not open his teeth. "Why does he always give trouble? You know what he's like...."

"O.K., give it here." The Chief Master stretched out his hand and one of the masters hastened to give him a crowbar. The Chief frowned with irritation. "No, not that. That's not what I want."

He reached instead for the submachine gun. Hurriedly and clumsily Ingus's master pulled the sling over his head. With a stab of the pain that was always lurking in his consciousness, Ruslan saw at last what happened when a dog was taken outside the wire. The pierced, blued-steel barrel casing was pointed downward, swaying above Ingus's head as though choosing a spot to thrust itself between the hemispheres of the sloping forehead and the ears that were laid back in fury. The muzzle was not thrust down, but something jerked rapidly inside the barrel casing and an orange-red halo flashed out around the slanting black muzzle, while out of Ingus's head ... out of the black-edged, lacerated hole spurted something hot and pink mixed with slivers of white. With a convulsive movement, Ingus stretched himself out with his head at the Chief Master's feet as though striving at last to lay the chewed hose on his boots.

As his master tried to straighten out the hose, Ingus's head was wrenched backward with it; there was still life in him—but only in his jaws, clenched in their last bite. His master threw down the hose and straightened up. He watched and the Chief Master and the other masters watched as the thick, gray snake thrashed around, flinging Ingus's head back and forth across the snow. But no animal could stand by and watch this; Ruslan could not watch it, and he flung himself down alongside Ingus. Even now, remembering how it had all happened, he could feel the plywoodlike firmness of the hose and the icy cold that set his teeth on edge. With a sinking heart he realized the hopelessness of trying to bite through that canvas neck—all he could do was bite some more small holes, from which stinging little jets of water came hissing out—while his ruff, his defenseless ruff stood up on end at the closeness of that black gun-muzzle, from which retribution was bound to roar out at any moment. And yet each time that he relived this unfortunate episode, he still could not feel that he was wholly guilty. The masters, after all, had done something that even humans should never do to each other, and Ruslan was not the only dog to follow Ingus's lead: Ruslan's lone misdemeanor lasted only a moment before the others joined in. Something large, gray and powerful flew over Ruslan, somersaulted and crashed heavily to the ground. Glancing sideways, he saw Baikal, always so placid and obedient; a moment later the cunning Alma flung herself at the hose, then the shaggy jaws of Dick—champion at guarding prisoners!—sank themselves into the hose right beside Ruslan, and in a moment the entire pack was biting and worrying the detested hose. Scorning duty and orders, all of them had cast off the restraints of obedience, and had forgotten their permanent fear of those black-muzzled guns, while the masters were forced to realize that they could only make their dogs obey them as long as the animals did not object too strongly. Right now they were insensible to the furious tugging at their leashes, which almost broke their necks, to the boots kicking at their stomachs and to the fact that the Chief Master himself was angrily waving a submachine gun and shouting at the others to get out of the way so that he could slaughter all these beasts with a single burst of fire—they were all useless now, anyway, and new ones would have to be found!

Coarse and inadequate though human language may be, dogs understand such things—but which of them was in a fit state to behave sensibly and let go? Now and again one of the dogs would raise his muzzle to the cold, infinite sky and howl—not with pain but with anguish at his own sin, at the poverty of a brain that could not cope with madness. Anyone able to interpret the dogs' supplication would have found it to be their eternal complaint—an animal's inability to penetrate the inscrutable workings of the human mind and discern its godlike intentions. For every beast knows how great man is, knows, too, that his greatness extends equally far in the direction of both Good and Evil; but that an animal, though prepared to die for man, cannot follow him all the way to the highest peak of Good nor beyond a certain threshold on the path to Evil—and that on that threshold the animal will stop and rebel.

Who could have imagined that Djulbars would save them all? Ignored by everyone, the only one to have kept calm, he suddenly stood up and stretched pleasurably as though preparing for a fight to defend his supremacy against all his rivals. No one noticed it when he bit through his leash—he was always chewing through it when there was nothing else to bite—but they all saw him trot forward with the loose end of his leash trailing in the snow. He walked right up to the Chief, faced the small, round, black gunmuzzle that was threatening the other dogs, and watched intently with his one and a half eyes to make sure that the Chief did not put his finger on the trigger: a small, scarcely noticeable movement but one that Djulbars recognized perfectly—the Instructor had demonstrated it so many times on the training ground—and that might be the last movement the Chief made in his life. The Chief dared not move his finger, knowing the temperament of this creature Djulbars, whom he had allowed to come so close. His self-confidence was shaken; this, too, Djulbars realized full well, and it was why he now allowed himself to take a small liberty: with his bearlike skull he nudged the black barrel and pushed it slightly upward. Although dumbfounded by this piece of impertinence, the Chief also approved of it; his face softened, and wiping his forehead with his mitten, he said:

"O.K., let the dogs chew the hose if they want to. There's plenty of water."

Then Djulbars, calm as ever, turned and went back to his place.

The dogs' attack of madness soon passed, and they all began to realize the real nature of this enemy they had attacked. It had punished them, and in a way they had not expected; Ruslan could not recall it even now without a shudder. He vividly felt again how he had choked on the jets of stinging cold water that spurted out of the holes in the hose, how the coat on his stomach—where it was so soft, long and fluffy—had frozen to the water-soaked snow, how he had twitched in pain as he tried to wrench himself free and found that he could not move. What a miserable bunch they were now, with their usually luxuriant coats sodden to the skin, suddenly reduced to such thin-looking, pitiful creatures, tearfully begging for mercy!

The masters used the same stream of hose water to wash them free from the icy surface, and then led them at a run back into the guardhouse, while some of the dogs, who could not even stand, had to be pulled along on sheepskin coats. There they all huddled into one corner, licking themselves and consoling each other for the disastrous incident. The masters pulled them apart, but they crawled back together again, for the law of their kind bade them comfort one another in misfortune and offer each other warmth and dryness in the cold.

There followed a terrible night, when they were led back to their kennels and each was left alone to reflect on his sin.

They could, of course, bark to each other through the thin walls, but this did not help to warm them up and they had nothing more to communicate than mutual recriminations and deathly forebodings. Many of them dreamed of Rex that night; they could even hear his voice, hoarse with cold and wind, as he lamented his solitude outside the wire and called upon them to join him. The older dogs remembered a certain Bairam whom Ruslan had never known, but who, it seems, had trodden that same path even before Rex, while the very oldest dogs recalled the famous Lady (the masters, for some reason, had nicknamed her "Lady Hamilton") who had been the first of all that ill-starred company; further back than Lady the history of the camp was lost in obscurity.

Next morning the masters came at the usual time and brought food, but they did not touch the dogs. They cleaned out the kennels, shook out the bedding in the corridor and talked in angry voices, grumbling about the Chief Master; some said, "He's fair, of course, but he's a brute," while others disagreed, saying, "He's a brute, all right, but he's fair." Then the Chief himself appeared and ordered the masters to feel the dogs' noses:

"Any dog with a warm nose can rest. The others are to go on duty. And that brute there is to stick close behind me, to make sure there are no more excesses like yesterday!"

Why did they take them out on duty on such a bitterly cold day? Why did they make them sit freezing in a semi-circle around the same hut which, though now quite silent, caused the dogs to have such painful memories of the previous day's episode? Surely it cannot have been simply to guard the huge box on wheels standing outside the hut, a wagon with high wooden sides that they always saw whenever there were deaths in the camp? Two wretched little horses, their eyes rheumy with the cold, heads nodding up and down like mechanical hammers, dragged the cart wearily through the camp gates and from hut to hut; then, loaded sometimes to the very top, it would bump away over the ruts and potholes toward the forest. The dogs knew that no one would try to rob or attack this cart or the freight that was carried in it. The cart never needed to be guarded by an escort: in winter it frightened people with the rustling and bony creaking of its cargo, and in the summer heat, when it was always accompanied by a thick swarm of flies, its nauseating stench made you want to run as far away as possible. If Ruslan had been able to put names to smells, he would have said that the smell coming from the cart was the stink of hell. Like all his fellow dogs, he could not accept the idea of death as total extinction, a state where there was absolutely nothing at all and no smells whatsoever. He did, however, have a vague idea of what the dogs' hell must be like: it was no doubt a huge, dim cellar where all of them, the Bairams and the Rexes, were chained to the wall. Huge hands gripped them by the muzzle, day in and day out they were whipped with leashes, stinging barbs were stuck into their ears and they were given nothing but mustard to eat. His picture of the human hell was rather less distinct, but no doubt it was not much fun there either, especially since people went there stark naked. The clothing of those who died was divided up among the living, and for a long while afterward Ruslan would confuse them with the dead, believing that the latter were still lurking somewhere nearby and might reappear at any moment. As far as he could remember, however, none of them had ever shown up again—they, too, were obviously confined to their cellar for a very long stretch, and there was as much likelihood of seeing them again as of meeting Rex alive and in the flesh. There was, though, something in common between these two hells—a mysterious, insistent terror and a dull, aching misery that could not be repressed or evaded once you had become aware of that grim secret.

So still and windless was the silence that even the cold could be heard: the crackle of steam issuing from the horses' nostrils, the crack of horse dung splitting, the creaking and groaning of the cart's woodwork. Their manes and tails white with hoarfrost, the little horses stood motionless; the driver on the box hunched his head gloomily into his shoulders, as oblivious to the loud clatter behind his back as if the objects being manhandled onto his cart were large, white, freshly sawed logs. Only once did he turn around to see whether they were overloading him today, then muffled himself up again in his black sheepskin coat.

The Chief Master, who alone was pacing up and down inside the ring of dogs and guards, had no need to seem so nervous. He could be satisfied that everything was proceeding calmly and that the dogs were carrying out their duty so patiently, although their rumps were freezing in the snow and their teeth chattering convulsively. Behind them they could sense burning eyes staring out of the little misted-up windows of the other huts; occasionally they could not restrain themselves and turned around—although in such extreme cold, when all smells were deadened, according to their canine understanding nothing could possibly happen. And nothing did happen, except when one of the two men loading the cart thrust himself forward, shook his fist and shouted at the Chief: "You'll answer for this!" But the other prisoner immediately stopped his mouth with a mitten and pulled him back into the dark interior. The Chief was standing with his back to the hut when this happened, and did not turn around.

All the dogs sat out this miserable spell of duty to the bitter end, as the Chief Master had wanted, and for this, presumably, they were all forgiven. No doubt if Ingus had been sitting there with them he would have sat it out and would have been forgiven, too. They were all very miserable at the absurd way in which Ingus had met his end; even Djulbars, his perpetual rival, could not make sense of it, and was convinced that it was his own fault for not having been sufficiently alert. The person who was most shocked of all, however, was the Instructor. After the dogs' revolt he walked around as though stunned. He began to confuse the dogs' names, and would say, for instance, to Baikal or Thunder: "Heel, Ingus!" and was amazed when they failed to obey him. He kept on thinking he could see Ingus everywhere, always seeming to notice him among the crowd, although the dogs had long since told the Instructor that Ingus was lying out there beyond the wire with a piece of canvas still clenched in his teeth. They had been obliged to cut it out of the hose, because Ingus's "immature" teeth had refused to loosen their grip and the masters did not feel inclined to smash his jaw with a crowbar.

Tired of waiting for his favorite to reappear, the Instructor thought up a game: he himself started to imitate Ingus. He actually developed some of Ingus's characteristics: he adopted the same dreamy, reflective air and careless behavior, and now when he ran around on all fours he displayed Ingus's special prancing gait. The Instructor became more and more obsessed with this game. Much oftener than before, he would say, "Attention! I will demonstrate!" and he did it better and better, until one day he put on an amazing act in the guardhouse: when arguing about something with the masters he suddenly dropped on all fours and barked at the

Chief. Still barking, he loped over to the door and pushed it open with his forehead. This made the masters laugh till they cried, but when they had stopped laughing and wanted to go and look for the Instructor—where should they find him but in Ingus's kennel. There he snarled at them from the doorway, growling and baring his teeth:

"I'm Ingus, don't you see? I'm Ingus," he yelled at them, speaking his last words in human language. "I'm not a dog trainer, I'm not a cynologist, I'm not even a man any longer. I'm Ingus! Woof, woof!"

It was then that the dogs for the first time understood *what he was barking about.* The soul of Ingus had taken possession of him—Ingus, who had always longed to break out and away, and was now calling on them to follow him.

"Let's run away from here!" barked the Instructor-Ingus. "Let's all escape! This is no sort of life for us!"

The masters tied him up with leashes and left him in the kennel for the night, but this did not quiet him; he made all the dogs restless with his frenzied summons, tearing at their heartstrings with a great, tempting vision of dense forests splashed with sunlight filtering through the branches and heavy with delicious coolness, promising them glades where the grass grew higher than the crown of their heads and the tops of their cocked-up ears, rivers whose water was as pure as tears, air that they would drink rather than breathe, and where the loudest noise in that air was the sleepy buzzing of a bumblebee; there in this promised haven they would live as free animals, inseparable, in one community according to the laws of brotherhood—and never, never, never again would they serve man! The dogs fell asleep and awoke again with a sense of longing, in happy anticipation of the long journey on which they would set off in the morning under the leadership of the Instructor—for it was spontaneously understood by all that he would be their leader, to which even Djulbars did not object, agreeing to take second place. Next morning, however, they saw the Instructor for the last time in the exercise yard. The masters carried him out, still bound, and tied him firmly into the backseat of a jeep. He continued to bark without cease, so they gagged him by stuffing an old forage cap into his mouth. The dogs sat in front of him, waiting for him to show them what he could do—perhaps he might push out the gag or free himself from the ropes, but he showed them nothing, only staring at them with tears running down his face. The dogs, too, were on the point of weeping; they had not suffered so much since, as dim-eyed, senseless little puppies, they had been torn from their mothers—until now, when a new life had just beckoned to them, when they had discovered a new aspect of the Instructor and loved him for it. Now this hope was dashed, and the only prospect that remained was the dreary, cheerless round of their familiar, everyday life. After that the training ground seemed empty and the dogs felt orphaned. The training ground ceased to be a place of excitement and pleasure, becoming instead a place of cruelty and sour bad temper. The new instructor, who arrived soon afterward, never demonstrated anything to them, but made much use of the whip....

AH, IT WAS BETTER NOT TO AWAKEN SUCH memories. Sighing noisily, Ruslan moved out of the lamplight onto the dark porch, where he took a long time to settle down, grunting and making the floorboards squeak a great deal before he was finally still, ears attentive to every sound as the world around him quieted down. As the night thickened into blackness and cold, more and more stars came out, glittering like the eyes of fabulous monsters. While he hated the moon so much that it somehow even smelled of carrion, he felt comforted by these bright, twinkling little lights. He could stare at them for hours, and had noticed an interesting fact about them: if you dozed off and then opened your eyes later, you found that the stars had moved. Thus he was able to observe the passing of time—and all his troubles were reduced to their proper perspective when measured against this celestial clock.

Divided, cut up by borders, frontiers, fences and prohibitions, our wretched planet flew on, spinning into the icy emptiness of space, toward the sharp pinpoints of those stars—and nowhere on its surface was there a place where someone was not keeping someone else behind bars; where one lot of prisoners, helped by other prisoners, was not guarding a third set of prisoners—and themselves—against the risk of taking an undesirable, lethally dangerous gulp of the bright blue air of freedom. In obedience to that law—the second after the law of universal gravitation—Ruslan guarded his prisoner, a sentry who would never be relieved from his voluntary post.

He slept with eyes and ears half open, never allowing himself to drop into insensibility. With his head resting on his paws, he occasionally twitched with fright, and another wrinkle was added to his steeply sloping forehead. His memories only released him from their hold when they were replaced by worries about the day to come.

4

SOMETIMES THEIR USUAL ROUTE WAS SLIGHTLY changed. When he reached the station and before turning off along the tracks toward the derelict passenger cars, the Shabby Man suddenly stopped, took off his mitten, scratched his cheek with all five fingers and said hesitantly to Ruslan:

"Shall we go in and see? Maybe they haven't forgotten about us...."

Ruslan agreed unwillingly, and they turned toward the station—not to its main entrance, but to a side door, on either side of which two blue boxes were fixed to the wall. Here the Shabby Man carefully scraped the snow off his shoes and gave a sidelong glance at Ruslan's paws to see whether they were clean. On the first few occasions he tried to leave his escort out on the street to guard his toolbox, but Ruslan would have none of it. He followed the Shabby Man up the steps, entered and stood waiting sternly for him inside the premises, disdaining to sit on the slushy, dirty floor. The air inside was thick and enervatingly hot, thanks to a round blue stove that took up the whole of one corner and helped to support the ceiling; in the barred windows, the one small pane that could be opened was kept tightly shut, while the two heads behind the counter were swathed in thick gray scarves. These astonishing heads chattered to each other unceasingly, performing actions of which each was the symmetrical mirror-image of the other as they caught sunflower seeds in midair from fists that moved up and down with machine-gun-like rapidity, tossing up the seed and then, on the downward movement, catching the ejected husk.

The Shabby Man sidled up to the counter, retrieved a crumpled piece of paper from deep down in his shirt front, smoothed it out and cleared his throat with a timid cough. For a long time they paid no attention to him until finally the symmetry was painfully interrupted, and one of the heads, frozen in the act of catching a seed, looked at him with a rigid, unblinking stare, while the other, who had been caught at the moment of spitting out a husk, wiped her mouth with the back of her hand and bent down under the counter, starting almost simultaneously to wag her head from side to side in a gesture of negation.

"Ah, well, I guess the letter's probably on its way," the Shabby Man said apologetically in answer to his own question, and put his scrap of paper back into his shirt front.

With time, the two heads learned this expression, and they would use it to rivet the Shabby Man to the spot as he came through the doorway, depriving him of a pretext to enter:

"Guess your letter's on its way!"

In fact he only went there to hear those words said, and for no other reason, but he would spend a long time strolling back and forth, hands clasped behind his back, reading everything that happened to catch his eye:

"A money order by telegraph—hear that, Ruslan?—costs seven rubles per hundred, but by mail it only costs two rubles. Well, I guess that's only right—time costs money.

A phone call to Moscow is two-sixty a minute. Pity I don't have anyone in Moscow to talk to. And I guess you haven't either, have you, Ruslan? Otherwise you might like to have five kopecks' worth and bark down the line to one of your friends."

He spent an especially long time in front of a poster from which stared a fat-faced, ruddy-cheeked young man with a sarcastic smile on his lips, holding a little gray booklet in one hand and with the thumb of the other hand pointing over his shoulder at a heap of various objects, among which Ruslan could vaguely recognize only two—a car and a bed.

"'I save and I look,'" read the Shabby Man, "'in my Savings Book...' Well, now! '... To see how my rubles are growing. If they are not spent, they earn five percent—It's the best deal of any that's going!' What lovely poetry. All those years in camp—and we never guessed. What did we save? We saved up days, yet it seems we should have been saving rubles. And five percent a year is not to be sneezed at, either...."

Ruslan, his head already at the door, would be baring his teeth in a frenzy of impatience and waving his tail—hurry up, time to go! But even when the Shabby Man did leave, it was not always to go to work. After these distractions the prisoner went to the station restaurant, gulped down a couple of mugs of that disgusting, foam-covered yellow liquid on top of what he had been drinking the night before, which made his breath stink like a cesspit, and then, only if he failed to find someone to talk to, would he finally set off for his work site. Sometimes he did not go to work at all; instead, he would drink a third mugful and go home, explaining guiltily to Stiura:

"Hell, couldn't seem to find a damn thing today. Nothing worth booking in—Ruslan will tell you the same. Still, we've enough to be going on with—should be a couple of planks left over from yesterday."

"Good," said Stiura approvingly, herself no great advocate of hard work. "Better to have you sitting at home than prowling around God knows where."

This slack behavior infuriated Ruslan. He could not bear irresponsibility. He himself was always preoccupied, always on the go: snatch forty winks, hunt for food at least once a day, escort the prisoner to work and back, run over to the platform to sniff out which dogs had been there and what had happened in the last twenty-four hours, visit the dogs in other backyards, find out the news, discover if any of them had any premonitions of change. Whereas these two humans slept as much as they liked, went no farther than the cellar or the hen coop to fetch their food, and nothing else bothered them—such as the fact that the train still hadn't come, that the work wasn't progressing and that Ruslan's days were just being frittered away to no purpose. But what could he do about it? Goad the Shabby Man into activity, urge him on? This had never been part of a dog's duties; it was the masters who set the tempo of work, who ordered the column to speed up to a trot or told the dogs to sit down in the snow. Ruslan was afraid that if he took this sort of thing on himself, he would be overstepping the bounds of the Service. There was only one thing to do: keep active and wait—to wait without losing faith, without falling into despair—and to husband his strength for the changes that were to come.

Meanwhile the snow was gradually beginning to look dirty and porous, and to give off a faint smell of something inexplicably delightful, something that caused stirrings of both hope and uneasiness. The air grew damper all the time, and on sunny days the roofs would drip steadily. Then they started to drip at night, too, disturbing Ruslan's sleep; thawed patches appeared in the middle of the street and the worn, splintered planks of the sidewalk began to show through. Only in ditches and where fences cast a permanent shadow did the snow still lie in heaps, but day by day they shrank, grew lumpy and oozed puddles of water that did not even look cold anymore.

So came the ninth spring of Ruslan's life—a spring that was unlike any previous one.

He came to learn that when the snows melt and the forest fills with sticky young greenery, the amount of live food increases too. Ruslan was no longer catching mice—perhaps because they had learned something from their tragic experience of the winter, or perhaps because he himself lacked the skill to grope for the little rascals in the thick, springy layer of last year's fallen leaves. To make up for this, the birds were much in evidence now, grown stupid and light-headed with their own singing, and the bigger the birds the more careless they were. Later, when their singing declined, he began to find their nests, low in the bushes or even right on the ground, in which there were some funny, longish, roundish pebbles, colored white or pale pink, or blue and speckled. Inside these pebbles was something warm and alive, and he reasoned that this must be good to eat, even though it was not running or jumping around. He would take them all into his mouth at once, crunch up the shells and suck out the warm, sticky liquid. The bird to whom these pebbles belonged usually tried to harass him by fluttering about right over his nose, but her indignant squawks made no impression on Ruslan—he knew a thing or two about diversionary maneuvers. But winning his daily meal by sheer robbery sickened him; a born fighter, he longed for struggle and contest, if necessary with mutual bloodletting. Catching a badger, for instance, was a real trial of cunning. Clumsy though this beast looked, Ruslan soon found out that a badger could never be taken by simply making a lunge for him. You had to use your brain, and above all you must not be impatient when the badger came out of his earth the first time, nor even the second time, for he was merely reconnoitering and might vanish into his lair in a flash; you had to let him be lulled by the quiet until he felt safe, and then his despair and confusion were all the greater when you blocked his retreat. No one had ever taught Ruslan any of this; there was much that he had not known about himself and was now learning, to his own joy and astonishment: firstly, he was discovering the attraction of catching your own food without having it brought to you in a feeding bowl, and secondly, he was finding out all the things he could do—creep up on the prey, flatten himself in the grass and ferns, hide for long hours and then pounce unerringly, like a flash of lightning.

Made reckless by his success, Ruslan on a sudden impulse dared one day to bring down an elk fawn; the risk lay not in whether he could bite through the thin tendons of the neck in time before getting a hoof in his flank, but in the fact that the mother elk was walking only just ahead along the path, and she caught him in the act. Rashly he attacked the elk doe, and our story of Ruslan's life came within an ace of ending right there, but a saving instinct told him that he had met a force from which it was wiser to retreat. He ran off with an exaggerated display of panic, though not forgetting to follow a circular course that did not take him too far away from his prey. He had to wait a long time, knowing that he was unforgivably late in reporting for duty, but he was in the grip of something stronger than himself, stronger than any feelings of duty or guilt. So he waited until the elk doe had abandoned her lifeless child—although he did not wait in order to eat it (there was no time for that) but simply in order to prove that he could show more patience than the inconsolable mother.

He also encountered the lords of the forest, of whose existence he previously had only a vague suspicion; they turned out to be very similar to himself, but how wretched they were in comparison! He was far bigger and stronger, and calculated at once that he was more than a match for one or even two wolves, but that he would have to run if faced with a whole pack. In fact, the wolves treated him kindly—they pretended not to notice him.

The wolves, however, did awaken one thought in Ruslan's mind: he might become a free wild animal like them, since he was quite capable of feeding himself by hunting. Ruslan did not know—and we, literate humans, do not always realize it either—that our surest safeguard against disaster is to stick to our proper way of life, to which we are suited and for which we have been trained. For he was already entering on the second half of his life, and throughout its first half he had grown used to an existence of complete adaptation to humans, whom he obeyed, served and loved. Most important of all was that he loved them, for no one on this earth can live without love: not even a wolf, a shark in the sea or a snake in a swamp. Ruslan was forever poisoned by his love, his pact with the human race—that same delicious poison that plays a greater part in killing an alcoholic than alcohol itself—and however blissful a hunter's life might be it could never surpass for him another sort of bliss: obedience to the person he loved, the happiness bestowed by his slightest praise. His hunting, to which no one had sent him and for which no one ever praised him when he was successful, he regarded merely as a job to be done that helped him to survive and keep his strength up. When the clock mechanism rang inside his brain—or rather, when the sun's rays striking through the treetops reached a certain angle—Ruslan had an inexplicable feeling that his prisoner was waking up and opening his eyes, and so he returned in answer to the call of duty, abandoning the hunt just when it was most interesting.

In the afternoon, as soon as he had escorted the Shabby Man home and waited for him and Stiura to reach for the bottle, he delayed not a minute longer before running off to the station. He alone continued to report for duty there, and Ruslan was now the only dog whom the railroad staff saw sitting on the empty platform or padding up and down the tracks. He would sometimes wait by the distant signal until darkness fell, listening to the humming of the rails, or meeting the freight trains and passenger expresses that smelled of smoke and the dust of far-off cities. When the trains roared past him or stopped at the other platforms, he felt furious at them and turned away, frowning involuntarily, then ran all the way through the station to the other signal and there sat for another long spell, meeting other trains that brought with them a faintly detectable whiff of the mighty ocean.

Sometimes when he was dozing half asleep the smells of distant places and the ocean he had never seen would disturb Ruslan, tormenting him with the seductive desire to set off at random along the railroad tracks, past one signal or the other, to run and run for as long as his strength lasted and until he finally saw what it was that had been beckoning him. But he did not know for how long he might have to run—a whole day or a whole summer—and then, while he was away, the train might come, the one and only train for which he waited.

From the height of the platform he could see the roofs of the town, spread out like a many-colored scab on the body of the landscape—there, too, was the bell tower of the church surmounted by a cross, which the setting sun always lit up with its last rays. It was at this hour, a time of melancholy and vague, disturbing thoughts, that Ruslan was often overcome with unease; he would begin to whine without cause, to sniff the air compulsively, and no sooner did he lay his head on his paws than he was surrounded by visions. They were strange visions. In all his years in camp they had only come to him in the darkness of his kennel, yet they were not ordinary dreams, because dreams never recurred so frequently and were never so memorable.

Sometimes he saw himself in a broad mountain valley, up to his belly in thick grass, rounding up a herd of sheep. The bluish, pink-tipped mountains were gradually fading into darkness, while a damp wind blew down from them, hinting at impending disaster; the sheep were huddling together and he was calming them by keeping up a low, hoarse, steady barking. Having completed a vast circle around the flock, he went over to a campfire where he sat down as an equal alongside the shepherds and stared long into the flames, unable to tear his gaze away from their mysterious, capricious flickering. The shepherds spoke to him just as they spoke to each other: "Ah, here's Ruslan.... Take a rest, Ruslan, you must have run yourself off your feet.... Have a bite to eat, Ruslan, we've left you your share...." And he accepted their respect as his due, because they could not manage without him. He would be the first to scent a wolf and would go to meet it as a sheepdog should—not just by barking to show off his keenness, but head-on with his teeth, feeling behind him the heat of the campfire and the presence of men who would always come to his aid....

... In the sultry heat of midday he was running down to a river with a crowd of little barefoot boys; they threw a stick into the water and he swam after it, thrusting aside the dense, still water, and afterward he would lie stretched out as though dead, his eyes closed against the sunlight, while the boys lay prone on their wet stomachs beside him on the sand as they ruffled his coat and prized out a tick that had fastened itself into his hot, drooping ear. Having bathed until they were almost blue with cold, the boys climbed lazily back up the hill while he followed at a distance, satisfied and proud that as long as he was there no harm could come to them—be it from a snake, a charging cow or a rabid dog.

... One blue, frosty morning in the Siberian taiga, he was floundering through a snowdrift to help his master, who was in trouble; sinking his teeth into the bear's rump, Ruslan held on with a deathly grip, and when he in turn was in mortal danger his master saved him by dispatching the brute with knife and rifle butt. After he had received his reward of the first slice of meat, dripping with warm blood, they set off home with their heavy prey, both wounded but roughly bandaged up, and both full of love for one another....

In all these visions Ruslan was aware of his love—for the shepherds in their shaggy black sheepskin hats, for the little boys, and for that slit-eyed, flat-faced Siberian hunter.

Where, though, had he seen them, whence did those visions come? At no time in his life until this spring had he ever seen mountains, or sheep, or a river shaded by weeping birches, or even any other animal larger than a cat. The only things of which he had direct experience were regular rows of huts, barbed wire, machine guns atop watchtowers and his master's left boot. Perhaps these visions, emerging unbidden from the deepest recesses of his memory, had been handed down to him by his ancestors—wolfhounds of the steppe, Eskimo trappers' dogs, shaggy-haired sheepdogs of the mountain valleys—who were his ultimate begetters and who, together with his stature, his strength and his courage, had also bequeathed to him everything that they learned in their lives. Why, though, should it be his lot to be troubled and tormented by other lives that he had not lived through? Or was he merely a link in an endless chain, and these disturbing visions were not destined for him but for the puppies that had been born to him or were yet to be born?

These visions, however, also gave him pleasure; he carefully cherished them in his heart, fearing to upset their flow, and amid the trials of his daily life he savored in advance the moment when he would be alone with those live pictures that so delighted him. At times he felt it was all happening to him in some past time—a time before he came to the camp, before the breeding kennels, before he was even conscious of his own existence—and he would dream about it as if it were a part of his own life of which he could be justly proud. Yet he sometimes also dreamed about a future that one day would undoubtedly come to pass, and these simple reveries brightened his life, imbuing it with a higher significance. These were the visions that kept him going: it was thanks to them that he did not fly off the handle with frustration, did not chew his own paw with boredom, did not starve himself and had only once placed himself in danger from his masters' bullets—which could have happened a hundred times to him, the son and grandson of sheepdogs whom fate had chosen for the role of herding two-legged sheep.

His master, who knew Ruslan well and knew his disposition and abilities, had never managed to fathom the chief riddle of his character, the secret held in his heart of hearts that Ruslan would not have dreamed of telling him even had he been able to. When the Instructor had said that the Service wasn't always right and that Ruslan should treat the whole thing as a game, he had come nearer to the truth, but only halfway. For the whole truth and the whole answer to the riddle of Ruslan's character lay not in his believing that the rules of the Service might in some way or another be wrong, but in that he did not regard his sheep as being *guilty* of anything, as did the Corporal and the other masters.

Certainly all his training told him that those people divided from him by barbed wire were wicked, hostile and bad; he was also used to hearing them called "sons of bitches," "swine," "bastards" and "fascists," and the whistling, hissing and roaring sounds made by these words were enough to make his hackles rise and a growl to start rattling in his throat. He well remembered, too, how when he was little more than a puppy these people had given him mustard to eat, had stung his ear with a needle, had fired at him with a big, stupid pistol, and had thrashed him across the back with a bamboo cane. They had, in fact, made his youthful days a misery and he had longed only to be grown up and get his own back. Yet when he did grow up and he could have brought any of them to the ground, he somehow never managed to find his tormentors among the crowd of prisoners—and he only wanted to find precisely those whom he remembered as having done him harm. Although similar to those particular villains, the other prisoners aroused his ire to a much lesser degree, and they were such cretins that his reactions to them gradually cooled off; try as he might to whip up his bad temper by recalling evil memories, his attitude became more and more one of astonishment as he realized just how stupid and pathetic their nasty little tricks really were, simply unworthy of the biped species. One of them tweaked your tail, while another snatched your food from under your nose—why, he wondered? Because they wanted to eat the food themselves? If so, he could have understood it.... But he had already begun to guess that they were not quite right in the head and that perhaps the masters had good reason to regard them as less than human. So what else could you expect of these poor, dim-witted creatures? How could you hate them? They were rather to be despised—because of their ceaseless squabbling, because of their fear of each other, because of never being satisfied with anything—and because they nevertheless submitted to intolerable treatment; because even at the very edge of the grave they lacked the spirit to fling themselves at their executioner's throat. But did Ruslan actually pity them at those moments when they meekly allowed themselves to be tormented or killed? To find the answer to that question, ask a sheepdog who has witnessed the slaughter of one of the sheep he has been so carefully guarding. He no doubt finds the sight depressing, but he does not love his master any the less for it. After all, the sheep never object—they hold out their heads with such enlightened resignation, such gentle weariness, such sublime sadness in their eyes as they offer their throats to the knife....

Did all the other dogs share Ruslan's feelings in this? He did not know. When the whole pack of dogs is zealously serving the common cause, they are unlikely to be frank on such matters. Perhaps Djulbars, the fiercest of the fierce, if given the chance, would no doubt have cheerfully bitten a prisoner to death. Yet would he? Who knows?... After the dogs' revolt he had been separated from all the others and permanently led around on a steel chain—the most glorious reward that Djulbars could have wanted! Now this fettered giant took every possible opportunity to shake his head, making the chain ring like a peal of bells as an audible reminder of his special status. Strangely enough, however, either because he had mellowed or because he had attained the ultimate, incontestable distinction, he somehow stopped showing his notorious bad temper. Indeed, why should he bother to wear himself out with ranting and roaring, now that the sound of his chain spoke volumes for his reputation?

Of course there were moments when the dogs loathed their human flock and feared them almost to the point of panic. This happened in the morning, when the main gates of the camp were opened and the camp guard handed over the column of prisoners to the outside escort squad. Seized by a nervous tremor, the dogs would grow hysterical, barking themselves hoarse. After all, they were only a tiny handful against this huge, hostile mob, which could easily have scattered and run in all directions—in the open fields or on the path through the forest. "Escape, escape!"—the thought was stamped out in the rhythm of their marching feet, exuded in the sweaty reek of their pants and armpits and it hovered over the column like a menacing cloud; awareness of it charged every hair on Ruslan's body with electricity until his coat was ready to crackle with sparks. Any moment now it might happen, at any moment they might break out in all directions—and he might do something wrong, make some fatal blunder. Gradually, though, the masters' calmness transmitted itself to the dogs; they were superior beings, and although they lacked a sense of smell, they knew everything in advance—so nothing would happen, or at least nothing that could not be kept under control. Sure enough, the smell that signaled the prisoners' urge to escape was soon dissipated, to be replaced by another scent, at first barely detectable, but gradually thickening and growing in pungency—the garlicky smell of fear. It seemed to come from low down, from legs that were beginning to stumble, refusing to run, refusing to carry bodies weakened and fettered by indecision. Ruslan felt relief in his heart, the dogs exchanged cheerful glances, letting their long tongues loll out, making no effort to conceal that they were panting from heat induced by nervous tension—the danger was past! It was just that these sick people had once again been deluding themselves with their invented notions of some kind of better life; it would soon pass—by evening, when work was over, there would be no more thoughts of escape and their only wish would be to get back into the warmth. Yet there was no end to the trials and tribulations that they caused their long-suffering nurses, armed with submachine guns, and their four-footed auxiliaries.

Rare were the patients who recovered, although on occasion Ruslan had noticed how they looked when they were discharged from this sanitarium: subdued, but emanating a steady aura of suppressed excitement. They left their ill will and rebelliousness behind them at the gate and always gave a weak smile as they made the same farewell remark, like a password, to the sentry:

"Here's hoping we never meet again!"

"So long!" came back the reply, as abrupt and clear-cut as a command, expressing certainty that the departing patient's disease would never recur. "Keep on the straight and narrow, and you'll be O.K.!"

And yet—just now, when an increasing number of patients were being cured, arousing hope that the inmates might abandon their unruliness, their fights and their stupid delusions and turn into a body of quiet, sensible people—they had all suddenly escaped at once. The thought of their perfidy no longer angered Ruslan; he merely pitied them for behaving so irrationally and for being unable to realize where they were truly well off. He, after all, had nothing but happy memories of the camp, and having now spent some time "outside," he could make some comparisons between the two. In the camp people had not been coldly indifferent to one another, but always kept both eyes on their neighbors' doings; what was more, a human being was regarded as something of the greatest value—of greater worth, in fact, than they knew—and that value had to be protected from the man himself by punishing him, wounding him and beating him if he tried to waste it by escaping. For there really is such a thing as being cruel to be kind: after all, they cut down the masts of a ship when this is essential to save it, and a surgeon has to slice up our body in order to cure it. Ruslan, too, had suffered—even to the point of bloodletting—in the harsh service of love; he had done his duty to that service day in and day out without respite, and in consequence it now seemed to him all the sweeter.

THE TRAINS, HOWEVER, WERE STILL AN UNCEASING disappointment to him—and at some point even the most ardent faith will burn itself out. If we try and correlate the long, drab, boring years of our human existence with the short and infinitely more eventful life span of a dog, then a true equivalent of the time Ruslan spent waiting for the Service to return would not be one winter and one spring, but perhaps four or five of our winters and springs. Hunting, for instance, very rapidly became an essential part of his life—he pursued it with a passionate intensity amounting almost to madness. In the twilit forest, with its voices and smells, he became a different creature, a stranger even to himself; and who knows? If it had ever occurred to the Shabby Man to pick up a gun one day and follow Ruslan into the forest, perhaps everything would have turned out differently between the prisoner and his canine escort: there in the woods, where the clumsy farce that we call life begins to seem so ridiculous, they might have abandoned those roles and become simply Man and Dog, in large degree equal to one another. But either because the Shabby Man never thought of it or because he had no gun, he just went on building his interminable dresser and showed no intention of changing his relationship with his escort. At about the same time, a longing of another, more intimate nature seized Ruslan with an unexpected, long-forgotten intensity—he sought out Alma and induced her to go hunting with him. Alma went with him as far as the edge of the forest, but there she stopped and turned back, for she had her own responsibilities now—her puppies, fathered by the mongrel with white-ringed eyes. If she had not had this commitment to keep her in the town, then perhaps the forest might have swallowed them both up and kept them forever.

All this is only guesswork. But if we had met Ruslan returning from the forest, coming down the middle of the road at a steady, swinging trot, we would have seen in him the mature perfection of a magnificent animal. It was obvious, too, from the glint in his yellow eyes that he knew himself to be in good shape, that he was proudly aware of the well-fleshed solidity of his paws, of the gleamingly healthy coat on his chest, and of how closely his collar now fitted his neck. When he entered the yard—with light and springy step, smelling of the forest, the earth and the blood of his prey—his hot breath terrified Stiura's little dog Treasure, who bolted under the porch, genuinely afraid that Ruslan's hunting activities might be continued in the yard with himself as the victim. He need not have worried: despite all the differences between them, Ruslan recognized Treasure as one of the same species, and he was forbidden by the law of his nature from killing his own kind—the favorite occupation of bipeds, so proud of their conquest of nature. To be more exact, due to his proud independence and preoccupation with his responsible job, there was no room in Ruslan's mental horizon for Treasure and his petty concerns. It never occurred to Ruslan that he might in any way be making Treasure's life more difficult—until Treasure himself pointed it out to him.

Stiura fed her chickens and went back indoors, leaving the door of the hen coop open. Ruslan heard the birds cackling and their gentle, sleepy murmur, and moved slowly toward the sound. He harbored no sinful intentions, but this particular breed of game was delicious to eat, as he had discovered when hunting wood grouse and heath hen. To his surprise, however, something suddenly blocked his path. He stopped and gazed in astonishment at the strange, ridiculous creature that said "Grrrrr" and bared its little teeth at him—at the same time wagging its tail and trembling in mortal terror. Weeping, Treasure implored him not to go any farther, and threatened him—but how? By telling Ruslan that he could only get into the hen coop over Treasure's dead body. This, of course, was not necessarily so: Ruslan would have simply flung him aside with a sweep of his paw, but he stopped all the same, hung his head in deep thought—and went back to where he had been lying. Perhaps he had reflected that there was such a thing as duty, for he had once been a sentry himself and could understand it when another dog had the same task, even when that other dog was so insignificant in appearance.

Treasure barely survived the experience. He flopped on his stomach, closed his eyes and took a long time to get his breath back, as though after an exhausting run. It was only from that moment onward that Ruslan really looked at Treasure, and he was amazed at the hellish difficulties of the little dog's existence, at the countless tricks of cunning and, indeed, the courage that life demanded of him. For Treasure lived in a land where a love of animals is sometimes expressed with the aid of sticks, stones and kicks, and in which he had about as many chances of surviving in one piece as there were centimeters in his height. Despite this, he was not just a nonentity who hastened to lick the hand that beat him; never once did he react by wagging his tail when a human threw something at him, but barked furiously and "chased" the offender at least to the corner of the street, although he never dared to go any closer and attack. The fact was that he had many qualities in which he would have measured up well to some of Ruslan's former comrades, and in some cases might have proved superior to them.

Ruslan saw his fellow guard dogs less and less, but he did not have to meet them to learn their news: the dogs' newspaper is written in the air and printed on lampposts and fences, and there was no end to the trivia and bitchy gossip to be read in it! Dick had turned to thieving again and had been beaten with the axle pin of a wheelbarrow used for carting manure, while the blinded Asa felt no shame in begging outside the bakery. Baikal had fixed himself a nice job in the meat department of a delicatessen, but if any other dog showed his nose inside the store, Baikal would tear him to pieces ... and so on and so forth. At first their petty squabbling infuriated Ruslan and drove him to despair, but in time he ceased to react to it. Their behavior was really quite natural and explicable in canine terms. The fact was that however they might strut around and boast about how useful they were in their new jobs, in reality they did these jobs thoroughly badly. And they weren't such fools as not to realize this. Their new masters kept them because they looked fierce, because of the metal in their voices, for the crystal-clear look in their eyes and their readiness to attack anyone when ordered—the only trouble with them was that to do anything they needed to be given an order, whereas the insignificant-looking Treasure, with his yapping voice, knew quite well what to do without having to be told. The guard dogs, for instance, only acknowledged one master and that had to be a man—his wife and family could not even come near the dog—whereas Treasure, although he acknowledged Stiura to be his mistress, was not loath to serve the Shabby Man, too, as long as he had some influence in the household. Treasure tactfully pretended not to notice any of the men who had lived with Stiura before the Shabby Man; he could also distinguish—better even than Stiura herself—between those women who were her true friends and those who were her covert enemies: each one was welcomed with the proper greeting due to her, or was not greeted at all; he could tell the difference between evasive debtors and importunate creditors—the former were to be enticed into the yard by cheerful, friendly yapping, while the latter were to be ignored at all costs. No one had ever explained all this to Treasure; he was simply doing what came naturally to him. All the former guard dogs would devour chicks without a twinge of conscience, and only after getting beaten did they understand it was a sin and never looked at the hen coop again; Treasure, on the other hand, though he might cast longing glances at the birds, never harmed a single chick, because he realized he would be the first to be suspected. Knowing that honesty was the best policy, he also knew that honesty was not enough—you had to be above suspicion. He understood that if you were unexpectedly allowed indoors, you might equally unexpectedly be chased out again; therefore you must neither loll around and outstay your welcome nor scratch your fleas when there was company present, and if the itching grew unbearable, you should start barking and run out-of-doors as if you had heard something suspicious. Treasure had learned his lessons in the school of life, where he had been thrashed and scolded, and frightened out of his wits by having tin cans tied to his tail. The experience had been tough and at times terrifying, but on the other hand it was his own, directly acquired experience; Treasure had never borrowed his intelligence from anyone else, had never been misled by the kind of training that humans dispensed purely for *their* advantage, and as a result he had kept his self-respect, his common sense, his equable temperament and an unfeigned sympathy for all the other mutts and underdogs of this world. He was a gossip and a braggart—none worse—but at the same time, he would not have dreamed of keeping it a secret if he knew where there was a tasty bit of food to be found, for instance. Yet Ruslan had never invited anyone except Alma to join his hunting expeditions. They, like all guard dogs, were used to always being given enough food and they had never had to share a feeding bowl—which, although it is upsetting to a dog at first, is a good lesson in solidarity.

Inscrutable are the ways of our four-footed friends, and it was by no means unlikely that if Ruslan had lived here for another summer he would have learned a great deal that he had never suspected during his isolated life in the Service, and he might well have woken up one morning to feel himself completely at home with this yard, this town, with the Shabby Man and Stiura. If Stiura, too, had persevered in her attempts to feed him with hot soup and bones, she might, no doubt, have been successful. He could not, after all, have kept up his suspicious attitude forever, since he might at long last have noticed that her broth caused Treasure no harm whatever.

Inscrutable, too, are our human ways. One day the two chatterboxes, who usually told the Shabby Man that his letter must be on the way, stopped saying that and instead handed him across the counter a well-thumbed, dirty-white triangle of paper. Ruslan's prisoner took it cautiously in both hands as though it contained something that might blow up in his face; Ruslan himself had learned a lot about such practical jokes in the training exercises to teach the dogs to be wary of inedible objects. Out on the street, the little triangle was unfolded into a tattered sheet; there was nothing terrible inside it, but it had an astonishing effect on the Shabby Man—he seemed to crumple up, and collapsed onto the step.

"Well I'm damned!" he said to Ruslan, who could see that, for all his shock, the Shabby Man's eyes had lit up. "You'd never believe it..."

What was it that could transform these dimwits so suddenly? You could shout and bark at them as much as you liked and they wouldn't move; perhaps it would have been more effective to give them each a scrap of paper covered in mauve squiggles, because this seemed a sure way to make them laugh and sob, bite their lips and slap their knees and then to display an unheard-of burst of energy. By all the rules—and for Ruslan anything repeated more than once became a rule—the prisoner should have stood up from that step, rushed straight to the station buffet and gulped down yellow liquid until he started to hiccup; yet instead he set off for his work site—and fast!—where he performed absolute miracles of conscientious hard work: the planks of wood flew out as he prized them loose, he did not even stop working to smoke, and when it was time to go home he positively galloped along the railroad ties with a huge bundle on his shoulder, singing a cheerful new song in time to his bounding stride:

> *"I save*
> *and I look*
> *in my Savings Book*
> *To see*
> *how my rubles are growing.*
>
> *If they*
> *are not spent,*
> *they earn five percent—*
> *It's the best deal*
> *of any that's going!"*

Now this was the sort of prisoner guard dogs only dreamed of—if only all prisoners were like this, life would be pure joy! Unfortunately their daily journeys were soon to come to an end. Twice more they went out and brought back a couple of good armfuls, after which the Shabby Man stayed firmly at home and started working on some mysterious task, which it was impossible to inspect because of the disgusting smell that came wafting out of the living room—a sickly, intoxicating reek that made your eyes smart and tickled your throat. Stiura flung open all the windows, so that the stench flooded out into the yard. Treasure sneezed and his eyes watered as he ran away to breathe more freely in someone else's yard, but Ruslan preferred to shift his post to the other side of the street. There were, of course, areas of the yard that were hidden to him from there, and under cover of that stink the prisoner might easily slip over the fence, but fortunately he always gave himself away by his voice.

Alone in the house from early morning, he could be heard bleating, grunting, groaning and asking himself threatening questions: "Who did that? I'm asking you—who primed that panel? So you won't own up, you rat? You should have your hands chopped off!" At other times, obviously satisfied, he would sing in a quavering, incredibly unpleasant tenor voice: "'Your wife, you see, has two legs, like a proper woman should!' . . ." When Stiura came home from work, they immediately started shouting at each other:

"How many coats are you putting on? Is that the tenth—or the fifteenth? Stop it, throw the filthy muck away, we can't breathe in here!"

"You'll see, Stiura!" he shouted triumphantly. "You'll see: you and I will rot away in our graves, but this dresser will last forever when I've finished French-polishing it—so my old bones won't need to feel ashamed!"

Later in the evening the two would fall into their customary silence; they liked to stand for a long time side by side on the porch, leaning on the railing, occasionally exchanging a few fragmentary words that died away into whispers, like a pair of conspirators. These two were up to something—and Ruslan racked his brains to guess what it might be.

Then one day he had a chance to approach and learn what they were planning. The Shabby Man's great work had been completed in a positive landslide of furious, last-minute activity, and he now sat there looking like a human fragment of that landslide—worn out but happy, with a pale, pinched face, slowly kneading a cigarette between his sticky fingers; under the torn collar of his shirt, stained reddish-brown, could be seen his sweaty, protruding collarbones. Her hand laid firmly on his shoulder, Stiura towered over him—majestic but a little sad, with a strange moist gleam in her eyes. She was wearing a smart blue dress, which Ruslan had never seen before, with short sleeves and trimmed with lace across the bust. The dress was too tight for her, and now and again she would pull it down and wriggle her shoulders. Stiura was also exuding a powerful smell of flowers.

"Still alive, eh, Ruslan?" asked the Shabby Man, as though Ruslan might not have survived the stench of that disgusting liquid. "Like it or not, it's time for you and me to say good-bye. I'm taking the train tomorrow—whoo-whoo!... Hey, maybe you could come with me? Don't suppose they'll ask you for a ticket. It's a long trip, to somewhere you've never been before. In three days you'll see more than you've ever seen in your life. How do you like the idea?"

As he said it, though, the Shabby Man was not seeing the train or the journey in his mind's eye, therefore Ruslan did not see it either, and so to the dog his prisoner's words remained no more than an empty string of meaningless sounds.

"The very idea!" said Stiura. "Taking a dog with you! And you don't even know whose he is."

"Don't know whose he is? He belongs to the government,

that's who. I'll take him home as a sort of souvenir. Other people brought back souvenirs from the war, accordions and stuff like that, so I don't see why an ex-con shouldn't bring back a trophy from the camps. Like to come, eh, Ruslan?" A crafty thought had crept into his mind, which was as yet unclouded with drink. "When we get home, we'll give people a treat, and show them how you and I used to walk together, with you guarding me. We'll show them just how we passed the time all those years. The folks back home have never seen anything like it in their lives—if I described it to them in the bathhouse they'd never believe me, they'd throw their wash-tubs at me. You must escort me strictly according to regulations: if I take one pace to right or left, you must growl; don't make any allowances—and if I make a false move, you can grab me by the leg."

This time the Shabby Man could see a very clear mental picture of it as he described himself and Ruslan walking together as prisoner and escort. As a result, Ruslan, too, was able to envisage it—and at last he thought he realized what was weighing on his prisoner's mind: he was longing to get back to the old times. Then Stiura witnessed something she thought she would never see: head lowered and wagging his tail, Ruslan came up to the Shabby Man and nuzzled his knee with his forehead. He pressed himself to that threadbare trouser-leg just as he used to rub against his master's greatcoat when he wanted to remind him that he was by his side and ever ready to come to his aid; but now he was also making a confession and a plea—which as a rule no guard dog would dream of making to anyone but his master: "I'm tired of waiting, too, but be patient. Be patient!"

"Look, he's beginning to get used to you!" said Stiura in amazement.

"Why not—he's a living creature, isn't he? It can't be easy for him to say goodbye. He must have some idea of what's happening. That animal has a good head on his shoulders. If I were you, I shouldn't kick him out after I've gone; he's a clever dog and he can still be retrained. Then when I come back—just see how he welcomes me."

His hand lay on Ruslan's closed eyes, smelling so strongly of that horrible, pungent stuff that it made Ruslan dizzy. This was too much of a liberty, even for a model prisoner, so Ruslan slipped away, went out and lay down outside the gate. He was, however, still full of kind thoughts for his prisoner, and he reproached himself for his absurd suspicions. He had been watching over this lost sheep for so long—and all the time the creature had been dreaming only of how he might return to the flock!

So for the whole of the next day Ruslan lifted his surveillance over the Shabby Man; finally the zealous guard allowed himself a completely free day. He went on a long and satisfying hunt, wore himself out running through the forest and lay in the sun to his heart's content, occasionally glancing down from a hilltop with a proprietorial air at the town spread out below: somewhere down there, in one of those cozy little houses, his chief quarry, his priceless treasure, was obediently guarding itself. The clock mechanism in his brain, however, was not switched off; it was still counting out Ruslan's free time, and at the uneasy hour before sunset, inexorable as ever, it gave Ruslan a faint signal, a scarcely perceptible jolt to the heart. Something was amiss; things were too good to be true.

As he came down the hill, he tried to think what might have caused his memory to give him a warning. Was it the unfamiliar blue color of Stiura's dress? Her sad, wet-eyed look of farewell? Yes, it was probably that tearful look—except that he now realized it had been a look not of farewell but of deception. For some reason, humans always felt a sort of remorse before committing some act of deceit or treachery. Ruslan remembered noticing a particular sadness in the eyes of prisoners whom the very next day he had had to chase when they attempted to escape: the villains had lulled him with that sad, caressing look in their eyes!

He did not have to turn off the main street, because their trail came out of an alley and down the main street toward the station. They had only recently passed that way, because the bitter reek of his polishing fluid and her strong flower scent had not had time to dissipate. They were obviously trying to cover their tracks with these smells—a clever plan, because they were stronger than tobacco. They had, however, made one mistake that would ensure that they did not get far: Stiura had put on new shoes, which like her dress were too tight for her, so that she found walking extremely difficult, and despite his nervous haste the Shabby Man had shortened his stride to keep pace with her.

He caught up with them at the very edge of the platform, and there much of his zeal for the pursuit faded away. He had expected to find them looking guilty and glancing around in fear, but instead they were just sitting hunched up and almost motionless on a bench. When Ruslan arrived, panting, they did not even notice him. Hidden from their view by a lamppost, he slunk along a silver-painted, wire-mesh fence and lay down behind their bench. From this position he could only see their feet—the Shabby Man was holding a tightly packed army duffel bag between his legs, while Stiura had kicked off her shoes and was wriggling her toes. He could, however, hear every sigh they uttered, even the slight hoarseness in their voices—and he quickly realized that they were not planning to escape together.

"Don't waste money on a telegram," she said. "I hate telegrams, anyway. But write me a letter with all the news. Force yourself."

"I'll write as soon as I arrive."

"Why write so soon? Look around a bit and find your family first. You may not even find them—anything can happen. And if you do find them, you won't be thinking much about me. But at least write before the month is out; otherwise I'll start thinking you've fallen under a streetcar."

"Sure, I'll write, I'll write," he said dully. "And you won't mope, O.K.?"

"I'll try not to. Anyway, there won't be much time to spare for moping. Didn't I tell you? We've been officially notified that our whole office is being moved to where your camp used to be. There's to be a big expansion program there. As of next month, they're going to run a bus service out to the old camp. So what with traveling back and forth every day and straightening up the yard a bit, I soon won't have much time on my hands. So if you come back and by any chance I'm not at home, you'll know where to find me."

As he listened he was scraping his shoe over the asphalt, and probably staring down at it.

"Stiura," he interrupted her, "I was lying, you know, when I told you I'd had a dream."

"What dream?"

"I said I'd dreamed that all my family were alive and were waiting for me. But there was no dream. I got a letter."

She froze into stillness and stopped wriggling her toes.

"Remember I told you I met a man in a transit prison who used to be a neighbor of mine? We traveled here together, all the way in the same railroad car. And we were in the camp together almost till the end—they released him six months earlier, because he had a disability. I'm not sure which of us was the luckier, though. His job was no use to him in the camps—he used to be a molder in a cast-iron foundry, and there's no call for that sort of work in prison. He spent the whole of his stretch on general laboring, did nothing but stack lumber all the time and got a hernia for his pains. I was put on lighter work 'cause I'm a cabinet-maker by trade. Sometimes the officers needed a piece of furniture made, and I can do upholstery, too—so I got by without knocking myself out. Never did a decent job of work for them, though—any old crap was good enough for those bastards!"

"Forget about it. You've got to start living again, instead of raking up the past. Well, what about this neighbor of yours?"

"Well, you see, I wrote to him—and I got a reply."

"The hell you did!" she said, deeply offended. "Why keep it secret, then? I'm not your enemy, am I? You should have told me right away you'd had a letter. Getting a letter makes it much better—it means you know for certain you won't be making the trip for nothing."

"No, I don't know that. I told him he wasn't to say I was alive, but just to drop a few hints, like: 'It does happen, you know,' and, 'Sometimes they do come back.' Well, he did as I told him. And they moaned and looked all upset."

"Of course they did! They were so excited, so thrilled."

"No, he didn't exactly say they were thrilled in his letter. But he did warn me that my eldest girl was studying at the university."

"Is she such a big girl? Well, congratulations. But what's bad about it? Why did you say he '*warned*' you?"

"Well, you know how students have to fill out a questionnaire before they can get into the university? And you have to say who your father is, where he works and so on. She can't say I've been in a prison camp since 1946—they'd never let her in. Any sensible kid would write, 'Father—Killed on active service at the front'—wouldn't she? And for all she knows, that's true. So it's going to look a bit funny if I suddenly show up as large as life. See what I mean? Mind you, I don't know for sure what she *did* say about me on her questionnaire. My neighbor couldn't find out—or rather, they wouldn't tell him."

"Those questionnaires aren't so important nowadays. They gave us a talk about it the other day at the office. They check them out, but they're not nearly so tough about them as they used to be. So don't worry. Tell me—what sort of welcome did your friend get when he came home?"

"Most of his letter was about himself. It was all in camp slang—I couldn't repeat it in front of a lady. It wasn't exactly a happy homecoming."

"Pigs! That's what they are—pigs!"

He gave a long-drawn-out sigh.

"I can understand their feelings, though. There they are, struggling with God knows how many problems already, and suddenly he turns up on the doorstep—an ex-con with a hernia. I don't know which of those two is worse. But it made me think: I won't go and drop on my family straight away, out of the blue. I'll lay low for a bit, and watch to see how they're getting on, without showing myself. And I'll call on my neighbor and talk things over with him."

"Much good his advice will be! I'm not stupid, you know, and I had my reasons when I asked you what sort of a welcome he got. He's frightening you on purpose, so that he'll have you for company. He has his own problems—it's not your job to sort them out. Look after yourself."

"No, that's how it used to be: to each his own. But now, since he and I have been in the camps together, we share our troubles and help each other out; it's different for everyone else—they can cope; they didn't go through what we went through."

From what was said, Ruslan deduced that the Shabby Man was already repenting of his attempt to escape, and would probably have turned back by now if she had not been egging him on—and how right Ruslan himself had been to resist the temptation of her bowls of soup! But either she was not being very successful in urging him to go or she did not really want him to go either. Whatever the reason was, the Shabby Man felt himself overcome by a familiar dread and growing weaker by the minute: the nervous movements of his shoe gave him away.

"If only it had happened earlier, Stiura! If only I'd known a bit earlier.... It's funny: when I got the letter, I was thrilled, but then I realized that I'd put so much of myself into making a life here ... into that dresser, for instance."

"What on earth's the dresser got to do with it? To hell with the damn thing...."

"No, I don't mean that. Earlier still."

"Earlier still? You mean when you were released? I'm sorry, but if you had turned up then and said, 'Any work you need doing, ma'am?' I'd have bawled you out and said, 'Shove off! There's all the money you need for your ticket. If you drink it all, don't bother to come back 'cause I'll kill you with the poker!'"

"When I said 'earlier still,' I meant I should have gone over the wall when I was halfway through my stretch. People did it, you know. Not all of them came back and not all of them got caught."

"I'll bet you'd have been caught."

"It wasn't getting caught that worried me—it was the thought of not making it all the way. The thought of dying in vain, like some wild animal in the forest. No one could make it home in one go, you had to make a stopover somewhere, but all I wanted to do was to get home—nowhere else. Just to see my family again with my own eyes. I wrote letters to them, but never got an answer. Later I found out they'd changed the name of the street, Goddammit—used to be Ovrazhnaya Street; now it's Marshal Choibalsan Street. And the number of the house was changed, too, because half the houses were burned down under the German occupation. I told myself: if I can only see my family, that's all I need. Then they can arrest me, double my sentence, even shoot me if they want to, I won't mind! But the problem was: where to stop on the way, who would give me food, who would give me a little cash for the journey—even though I would have worked for it? You can't knock on every door—and when you do, will there be a kind soul behind it? If only I'd known that you were living right nearby, almost in my pocket so to speak ...!"

"You're talking nonsense again," she said with the same boiling irritation that heralded one of their quarrels that always ended in shouting. "Now that's all a lot of crap. Want me to tell you? Sure I was living here—but with somebody else. O.K., I would have let you in. And I'd have fed you and given you a drink. And you could have slept in the warm. But I'd have gone straight and told the police—they were on duty here at the station day and night."

"Would you really have gone to the police?"

"What else could I have done? The neighbors are all

good Soviet citizens; how can you keep anything secret? Yes, they've made us into a nation of stool pigeons—what a lovely thought."

"Who did that, Stiura? Who could do it?"

"Don't ask me, because I won't tell you. I've told you what would have happened and that's enough. I told you so as you'd know that if you had tried to get away earlier, nothing would have come of it. Does that make you feel better? Now you can cheer up and go."

The train had already come into sight in the twilit distance. A few travelers were moving to the edge of the platform and a warning bell rang in the station.

Stiura was the first to get up, and stamped hard on the ground with her shoes. The Shabby Man stood up slowly as though ungluing himself from the bench, rising with the same reluctance in his legs that a prisoner feels when forced to leave a campfire and go back to work in the cold. He even looked as if he were freezing, since he was wearing his winter cap and overcoat and was wrapped up to his ears in a scarf. She helped him with his duffel bag and hastily kissed him three times. He embraced her convulsively, letting the cord of his duffel bag slip down from his shoulder to his elbow. No sooner had he mounted the steps than the couplings jerked all along the train and the car started to move. The Shabby Man turned around—his face white with fear, sweat on his temples, an insane look in his eyes.

"Stiura!"

"Don't worry." She walked alongside the car. "I'm still here. Hold tight."

His tongue lolling out with the heat, Ruslan watched them go. Though we in our patronizing way may call dogs our "brothers," we still qualify them as little or younger brothers; but if one of us bigger, older brothers had been in Ruslan's skin and doing his job at that moment—what would we have done? Would we have run after them? Would we have caught up with him and pulled the prisoner to the ground? Would we have flattened him on the asphalt, growling furiously? The step on which the Shabby Man was standing had already drawn level with the station building, Stiura had tired of following the car and turned back—black and flat as a target, bearing the scarlet disc of the setting sun on her shoulder—yet Ruslan still lay in his place and waited, certain that the Shabby Man was not leaving, was not lost to him. When the duffel bag flew through the air and flopped onto the ground, he could turn away without bothering to watch as Stiura ran up to the Shabby Man, swearing as she helped him to his feet, and as they embraced again on the empty platform as though meeting after a long separation.

She helped him to a bench and sat him down, standing in front of him, shaking her head and frowning with vexation. Then she took off his cap and unbuttoned his overcoat.

"There now, sit awhile. You stupid man—you should have handed in your ticket before the train left. O.K., we'll pretend you went away and came back again. Now rest and take it easy."

"No," he said, breathing jerkily as though he had been winded. "We'll say that I never meant to go at all. Where was I going, anyway? Who was I going to? You must understand me . . ."

"I understand," she said.

They took a long time to return home, stopping to sit down on nearly every bench outside other people's yards on the way. The Shabby Man was carrying his cap, Stiura carried her shoes. Ruslan followed them at a considerable distance, unnoticed by them. He was not particularly pleased at this return—if only they knew how much extra trouble this was going to cause him! Something would have to be done with the Shabby Man; he was worn out, he had lost faith and had given up waiting, so he had tried to go away—only to realize that it was useless. And strange things were happening in the place where Ruslan wanted to take him, the only place where his prisoner could find the calm and orderly life he longed for. Since the day when he had picked up his master's trail at the end of the main street, Ruslan had not been back there; indeed it had not even occurred to him to wonder what was happening in the old camp. While guarding a single prisoner, he had neglected something much more important—and by certain mysterious, subtle threads that important thing was for some reason linked to Stiura and to something she had said at the station. That was why he had suddenly been reminded of the camp while lying behind that bench on the platform.

Till late that night he listened to them sitting noisily over a bottle, while the Shabby Man kept on tearfully trying to explain something; nothing would calm him down or stop his interminable flow of reminiscences and arguments.

How many times in recent weeks had Ruslan observed loaded flatcars at the siding and seen the crane lifting up pallets carrying bricks, long gray girders, panels of sheet metal and huge boxes marked with black writing; all this had been loaded onto trucks and driven away up the familiar road that led to the camp. For appearances' sake he barked at the trucks; no one ordered him to, but he was on independent duty now and could occasionally give himself orders. Sometimes he followed them to the end of the street, but never once did it occur to him to chase after them to their destination. Had he been capable of blushing, he would have gone crimson from his nose to the tip of his tail and turned smoking hot with shame!

Morning found him out on the road, which had changed greatly since he had last gone that way; it had been widened, and from the edge of the town onward the road surface was covered with fine, light-colored gravel. Where once the road had curved around the edge of a gully, this bend had now been straightened out by a newly made embankment, on whose sloping side a bulldozer was rumbling back and forth. Through the forest it ran like a river, the tree-grown edges having been widened and pushed back, and it would have been a pure pleasure to run along it, had not the gravel felt so sharp to Ruslan's paws. Alongside the road, however, among the trees, there ran several fine trails that had been newly cleared of fallen tree trunks and branches; these paths sometimes led off into a thicket, then curved back again to the road, which was never out of sight for long. In any case Ruslan would have found it hard to lose touch with the road, because it gave off such a powerful smell, a mixture of lime and engine oil.

When he reached the camp he was completely stunned. The sight made him sit down and hang out his tongue in alarm and perplexity. He had never imagined seeing anything like it: right across the open fields, stretching far beyond the old camp perimeter, were row upon row of single-story gray buildings; in some of them the tall windows were already glazed, some were still just empty spaces beneath newly erected roofs, while others were no more than a series of uneven posts sticking out of the ground. He began counting: six, then another six, after which he lost count. Ruslan could only count up to six, because the regulation column of prisoners had been lined up in ranks of five; if a sixth had sneaked in, the masters had said "too many," and ordered him into the next rank. So it was simpler to say that there were "too many" new buildings. Strangely enough, however, practically none of the old prisoners' huts were left, except two or three, and they all had broken windows. The masters' barracks were still there, also the storehouses and the garage, but of the building that had housed the dogs' kennels there was no sign.

He ran to find it—not a trace, not a smell. The people walking around the place, who cheerfully called out to him, had so messed it up with their bonfires, pools of cement mixture and heaps of slag that it was impossible to say even approximately where the kitchen, the exercise yard and the training ground had been. He even had the impression that the place was not a camp at all any longer but some other institution, and the camp had been moved somewhere else. Such a move had, in fact, happened twice during his lifetime. At one camp, the forests had gradually been thinned out and cut back so much that the work columns had to be marched over a long and ever-increasing distance to the logging sites; at the same time the huts had filled up with more and more patients coming for treatment, so that in the end a full-scale relocation had perforce taken place. The whole enterprise had begun again at a new site, starting literally from the driving of the first stake. When everything had settled down and was functioning properly, it turned out that the new camp was much more spacious than the old one, and that the dogs, for instance, had better living quarters—clean kennels, a nice, warm guardhouse and heaters installed in every sentry box; even the inmates could not complain about the new punishment cells, which were made of reinforced concrete and had room for many more of them than the roofless wooden cage at the old place. Even so, by last summer the overcrowding had grown to be as bad as ever. Because of it, everyone's nerves were on edge and the prisoners began to complain in loud, angry voices; more and more frequently they would gather in crowds, refusing for a long time to disperse. Even the dogs realized that another move had simply become a necessity, otherwise something would happen before long. Sure enough it did happen—and the escapers had not been found yet.

No, it was still a camp and not something else. When they had moved in the past, the old site had always been completely leveled, leaving behind nothing but a few dead ashes and filled-in latrine pits. Ruslan had to admit he was glad that this time they had decided not to move but to build a bigger camp on the same site. The only thing that worried him was that the new buildings were being placed dangerously close to the forest, and some were actually being built among the trees; if the machine gunner on the watchtower spotted someone trying to escape, he would have no time to take aim before the runaway had vanished into the forest. And by the way—there were no watchtowers! Nor was there any barbed wire to be seen—the wire from which everything had begun, the wire for which that first stake had been driven in!

He decided that they would string up the wire later, when everything else was ready and in its proper place. Perhaps, too, they would cut down a lot of the trees surrounding the camp, so that there would be good, all-around observation. Where, though, would it go, the double perimeter fence of barbed wire? He could not figure it out. The camp, as he saw it, had started to expand in all directions, and the wire would have to be moved farther and farther back, until it was enclosing the whole forest, and then the town and the station—and finally every bit of the surrounding landscape that Ruslan had come to know. The thought was breathtaking—why, then even that damned moon would be in the line of fire and the masters could shoot it down or lock it up in solitary! That would be wonderful; the light from the camp floodlights was quite adequate—it was also less upsetting and it made fewer dark corners.

What was the nagging thought that still worried him, which still did not square with his scheme of things? He knew that the world was a big place and that in whichever direction you might go, there was always more of it to come. He remembered how his master had driven him away from the breeding kennels in the cab of a truck and had allowed him to look out of the window. What a long drive that had been and how much there had been to see! So if the world was as big as that, how many stakes would have to be driven in, how many of those heavy coils of barbed wire would have to be unreeled? Perhaps ... perhaps the time had come to live without any barbed wire at all—and the whole world would be one huge, happy prison camp?

He sadly decided, however, that it wouldn't work. Everyone would wander away where he pleased and the guards could never keep track of them all. It would be impossible to give every person his own guard dog. There were an awful lot of people and not enough dogs; he didn't count mongrels, of course—there were more than enough of those—but real dogs, fit for the Service, who had been selected, bred up and trained. Only after proper training was a dog capable of teaching something to humans, who bred without selection and never learned anything. Besides that—sad though it might be—there had to be a place where you disposed of certain dogs who forgot the rules of the Service and certain unreliable prisoners; since it was forbidden to use firearms in the accommodation zone, where would you take them if the whole world was a camp? It came down to this: barbed wire was indispensable. But where would it go? Where it was needed—that's where it would go!

So all was well. He started back, satisfied with what he had seen, even though he was late; he had not had time to go hunting, and somewhere along the way would be the moon, which no one had yet managed to shoot down. Clearly the moon did not want to come out tonight, but something was lighting his way all the same: he could easily make out the path, the bushes and the trees. Stopping to relieve himself, he looked up at the sky and saw the stars. It was they who had decided to shine for him tonight—good, let them shine. He ran on, and the stars ran with him. When he stopped, the stars stopped, too, patiently waiting for him. He knew this trick of theirs already, but it always thrilled him. He stared at the stars with gratitude, meaning to give them a friendly bark—when at that moment it suddenly came to him that the train, which he and the Shabby Man were waiting for so longingly, was soon due to arrive.

A bright flash lit up his brain and showed him a vision, the most delightful of all his visions. He had never seen the sea, but the salt of our primal mother was dissolved in his blood and carried with it ancestral memories of the menacing roar of the ocean, rolling its endless waves upon the gray, shingly beach, while the smoking wave-crests surged into the air like fountains and white birds wheeled in the dark sky, heralding disaster. His master's crook and white cloak lay on the shore, alongside his rope sandals and the knapsack with his bread, while his master was swimming beyond the line of surf. Though exerting all his strength, he could not overcome the roaring undertow of the waves and he called for help. Ruslan barked to him: "I'm coming, hold on a little longer!" and flung himself into the thick of the water, which rose before him like a solid wall. He thrust his muzzle into it, blinded and half-deafened, hearing only the glasslike scrunch of pebbles, and when he could hold his breath no longer, he surfaced and gulped air into his lungs. Then he swam toward his master, full of pride and happiness, flying high on the crests and slithering down into the troughs, nearer and nearer to his master, at one moment losing him from view, at the next catching sight of his head amid the raging elements.

Shaking off this vision, Ruslan trotted on. Other cares were burning him and driving him on now: he must keep a better watch on the station, he must alert the other dogs. He was nagged by a doubt: would they believe him? For a long time now his attitude of unflagging zeal had only antagonized them. Themselves soiled with corruption, they were all too ready to suspect him of being corrupted, too: he had already overheard a rumor that he was *serving the Shabby Man*! No slander could be more vile! If you looked at things calmly, however, it might be said that he had lowered his standards: he had nuzzled a prisoner's knee—the shame of it! In a sudden access of guilt, he asked himself: on the very eve of their return to the Service, could he be said to have transgressed its rules? Had he given his allegiance to anyone or anything but the Service? No, no and no again. He had taken no food from anyone, had obeyed no one's orders, had never truckled to anyone. He had never befriended strangers, had never had any contacts that did not befit a dog who belonged to the Service. Just a moment, though—what had happened between him and Alma? Yes, with Alma—without orders, without a leash and without the masters, who were always supposed to be present on such occasions. Good Lord above—nothing had happened between Ruslan and Alma! There had been a tremulous attraction, a heedless surge of emotion, they had run alongside one another as though harnessed together, shoulders touching—but she had been thinking all the time of her puppies, and her puppies were her sin and she must answer for it as best she could. True, Ruslan had felt very sorry for Alma, but he himself had a clean conscience.

Gentlemen! We, the lords of creation, can feel satisfied that our efforts had not been in vain. A strong, mature, pureblooded animal, running at night through the deserted forest, felt upon himself the cruel, ugly though invisible harness that we have made for him and counted it a joy that this harness was nowhere too tight, nowhere chafed or scratched him. If anyone were to undertake to fill out Ruslan's official questionnaire concerning his political reliability—and there was a time when dogs actually had such questionnaires, though they have since disappeared along with all the other records into the cellars where archives are kept "in perpetuity"—it would be a gleaming, unspotted piece of paper, with nothing on it but deletions, no entries but that favorite word of ours: "Not." He was not. Did not have. Did not belong to. Had not taken part in. Had not been interested in. Had not been subject to. Had not wavered. If there is justice in heaven, then the great Service should have taken that into account and should have summoned him, the first of the first, as he sped on toward his duty, fearing to be late.

And the Service did summon Ruslan one more time.

5

HE HAD WAITED—AND WAS REWARDED. ANYONE who waits with such single-minded devotion is always rewarded in the end. Nor was the good news brought to him by someone else who by a lucky chance happened to be there: that morning Ruslan himself was on the platform when the red light began to glow and a dirty, wheezy little switching engine, tender first, pushed the train of gray-green passenger cars into the siding.

The wheels were still clicking over the rail joints, a hissing sound could still be heard beneath the cars when an astonishing, incredible horde of people started pouring and tumbling out of the doors with a great deal of shouting, hubbub and laughter, with much clattering of boots, shuffling of shoes, banging of suitcases, trunks and backpacks. Ruslan was almost stunned, blinded and overwhelmed by a wave of stupefying smells; he jumped up and ran, barking furiously, to the other end of the train—something that he had never done before, but then never before had he been called upon to meet such a huge party nor one that was so strange, noisy and slovenly, half of it, for some reason, made up of women.

The Service had come back, though—and Ruslan was ready for it. In a moment he was transformed: flexible, alert, his yellow eyes sharp and keen; the hairs on his ruff stood on end like a collar, while ears, stomach and the tip of his extended tail quivered with a low metallic growl. If he allowed himself to misbehave slightly, it was out of joyous excitement: he grabbed and tugged at a backpack, whose owner, roaring with laughter, pulled it away from him by the straps, and although he almost yanked Ruslan's teeth out with it, this did not annoy him. He jumped up with his forepaws on the men's chests and licked their salty faces until someone stuffed the corner of a prickly army blanket into his mouth—and this did not upset him either, although it took him a long time to spit the wool out of his mouth. They had all come back! And what's more, they had come back voluntarily! They had realized after all that there was no better life beyond the forests, far away from the camp—which, of course, the masters and the dogs had known all the time—and they were obviously delighted at their discovery.

Ruslan, however, did not forget his duties, which were to check that everyone except the uniformed conductors had left the cars, and to make sure that the passengers lined up two paces back from the edge of the platform, where they must wait until the masters arrived.

The masters were disgracefully late, especially since in the old days they had always been standing there long before the train pulled in, each one with his dog, opposite the door assigned to him. There, on the concrete platform, the train escort had handed over the incoming batch of prisoners to the camp escort; the new arrivals were then made to sit down in line, hands clasped behind their necks, while the masters walked up and down between the rows calling the roll, counting and recounting them, and examining their luggage. Anything that could not be carried was removed and loaded onto a truck, and if any of them objected to this, the dogs would intervene without orders.

On this occasion, however, nothing seemed to be done according to the rules: they did not sit down or pile their baggage alongside them, but simply picked up their belongings and surged off in a disorderly crowd. This upset Ruslan very much, but he was reassured when he saw that they obviously had no intention of trying to escape, that they were not jumping down from the platform, but were taking the familiar route—down the steps and into the square. His only concern was to see that the party did not get too strung out, for which purpose he had to prod a few people with his paws or his muzzle. Who had been the first to think of this method of urging on the stragglers? No doubt it was Ingus. Who else could have dreamed up anything so stupid? The men he prodded did not like it at all; he was, after all, urging them on so that they would get into the warmth all the sooner, but they shied away and shrieked in terror—as if the dogs' only pleasure was to bite, whereas they were in just as much of a hurry to get back indoors. Later, Djulbars had adopted this method, and of course the swine had ruined everything as he always did—but then he was Djulbars!

Out on the square, around the railing of the little central plot of grass, they all gathered into a crowd again, put down their luggage and turned to face the station. There on the steps stood two short men wearing identical gray suits, with something red at their throats; one was fat, the other, thin. The fat one only smiled, his hands clasped behind his back, but the thin one put a pair of spectacles on his nose, unfolded a piece of paper and talked to it for a very long time, occasionally flinging his hand into the air as though throwing a stick to be retrieved. Two or three times, after a pause, he repeated the words: "And so you, young builders of the cellulose fiber factory..." As soon as he had finished and was folding up his piece of paper, the fat man unclasped his hands from behind his back and started to smack his palms together. Everybody else started to slap their own hands, too, and to shout "Hurrah!" while some at the very back shouted "Boo!" and seemed very pleased with themselves for this. Then one of the newcomers mounted the steps, put his suitcase at his feet and also took out a piece of paper. He did not talk to his paper for quite so long, and repeated a slightly different phrase: "And so we, young builders of the cellulose fiber factory..." All these strange words tickled Ruslan's ears—rather like the words that the Shabby Man liked to shout after he had been at his bottle for a while: "sandalwood," "palisander," "White Finns..." By the way, thought Ruslan, he might like to be here. Shall I go and fetch him?

There was, however, no time for him to go—the people had finished talking, waving their arms and smoking; they picked up their luggage from the ground—luggage that no one had examined!—and began to form up into a column. This was a surprise—and a pleasant one: they were forming a column on their own initiative! Although they had so far broken almost every rule, they had at least remembered the most important one of all—not to move in a disorderly crowd but in a proper column. Feeling very satisfied and immeasurably proud that he alone was escorting such a large party and knew where to lead it, Ruslan took up his position on the right-hand side near the head of the column, and set out on the road—a road whose end he was not to see.

The column headed out onto the main street. Moving at a leisurely pace, it flowed over the permanent ruts in the street, while its thousand boot-soles trampled the wayside plantains and raised a cloud of pale, clay-colored dust that settled on the sparse poplar trees and sharp-pointed tops of fences. Somewhere amid the ranks a guitar tinkled and accordions began to wheeze, at which a girl wearing men's pants and with short-cropped hair like a boy eagerly ran out ahead, turned to face the front rank and started to dance backward, neatly and deftly, singing in a raucous, cracked voice:

> "I stepped out on the road so smooth,
> Along the road so wide-oh!
> My lover wants to have his due,
> But I won't be his bride-oh!"

This was an unheard-of breach of regulations, but since it was being committed by a woman, Ruslan was not sure what to do. In the columns he had escorted in the past, women had been an exceptional rarity. They had never given any trouble, except that they were more prone to lag behind and had to be made to catch up; on the other hand they never tried to escape, so on balance he felt indifferent toward them. He decided to leave this girl alone, especially as her performance was not causing the others to break ranks. The accordions were bellowing away at full blast, the girl twirled around on her own axis so that she ended up again facing the front rank and dancing backward, smiling all over her high-cheekboned, sunburned face. She was still singing but now quite inaudibly, because the men's voices were roaring out their own nonsensical song:

> "Ruble for the hay, the cart costs two,
> Ruble for the ride for me and you—

*Beans and peas, peas and beans,
Load it to the top with peas and beans..."*

Farther down the column they were singing about the soldier and his girl who had to part because:

*"He's been ordered to march westward
But eastward she must turn her steps..."*

While from the back came the strains of a song about the old tomcat who "... sat on the mat, eating bread and mutton fat..."

Windows were opened along the street and people looked out—some as though stunned, others with a mirthless grin of amazement. In some front yards, women with their long skirts hitched up for gardening straightened their backs and stared, shading their eyes from the sun. A white-haired old man wearing a patched army tunic walked over to his low fence and watched silently and impassively with his faded blue eyes. His hands, grasping the handle of a spade, were covered in large veins as dark in color as the spade handle, as dark as his lined, weather-beaten face, while his elbows and open neck were thin and white, the skin underlain by a network of little blue veins. The old man moved his lips for a long time before stroking the top of his head and asking:

"Where are you boys from? You from Moscow? Or from someplace else, maybe?"

"We're from all over, granddad," they replied. "Moscow, Bryansk, Smolensk. Guess you never saw people from so many places before."

"Sure, I've seen 'em," said the old man. "All sorts used to

go down this street. Some from Bryansk, some from Smolensk, too. Only they didn't sing."

He gave a gap-toothed smile and hobbled back to his flower beds.

And so the column marched on, yelling, laughing, exchanging shouts with the bystanders—which made Ruslan less than happy. He did not like these new rules, which upset the grave solemnity of the Service. He knew, however, that he must be patient; the newcomers' loud, nervous and silly behavior would very soon cease, just as they would soon stop looking so cheerful and fat-faced. Before long they would all be looking subdued, foreheads and eyes appearing disproportionately large in thin, pale faces that would seem to glow with an inner light. He only regretted that he could not tell them the good news: they clearly did not know what a spacious camp had been prepared for their benefit, what big, wonderful, new huts awaited them, huts in which they could all fit easily—well, maybe a few would have to be packed in a bit tightly—and that there was no barbed wire yet, although this did not matter because they themselves would soon be put to work stringing it between the posts. Once the wire was in position they would never again dare to cross it, nor even to approach it, but it would be their very own wire, because it was always the prisoners' job to put it up.

Suddenly he noticed that the other dogs had all started to converge on the column from every direction. They came running out of alleyways and yards, jumping over fences, all similar in looks—with smooth, black backs and fluffy yellow fur on their stomachs, and all with identical grins of joyous anticipation; even their tongues, it seemed, were all hanging out on the same side. All were his erstwhile comrades: Djulbars, Yenisei, Baikal, the inseparable Era and Cartridge,

Trigger and Breechblock, Dick and Caesar, Whitey, Daring, Graycoat, Alma and her boyfriend with the white-ringed eyes—hey, what was that civilian doing here? He was not the only civilian to turn up; with him came a whole horde of mongrels—all those nondescript Treasures, Spots, Patches, Busters and Fidos, along with several who had no names at all. Last to appear was Lux (whose masters never called him anything but Luxy)—a creature Ruslan found repellent, who looked like a bitch and was rotten to the core. In fights, Lux immediately rolled over onto his back or whined to Djulbars, who treated him as his protégé. He had earned this status by pretending to bite Djulbars's fleas for him, of which he had none, but Lux put on such a convincing act that everyone thought they could really see them. That was how he had kept his place in the pack—by playing the toady and the fool. Just now he had been rolling in the dust, then jumping up and snapping his teeth as though catching a flea in midair. This performance was the cause of his being late, yet because of it the other dogs greeted him with smiles and wagging tails, whereas they seemed not to notice Ruslan at all. He was not the first to encounter this perverse instinct of the mob: it adores a clown yet spurns a hero.

As he ran forward to take up his leading position as the senior dog, Djulbars gave Ruslan a friendly nip on the shoulder. Ruslan turned away with a growl; he had not forgotten the woodpile and Djulbars's revolting display of servility to that puny little man with the motorcycle. He was not envious by nature, but now he bitterly envied Djulbars—the swine always took first place in the column and Ruslan only second place, and now once again he was obliged to drop back. He ended up trotting alongside a young man wearing new shoes with thick rubber soles—how that rubber stank! Yet he could not help feeling a warm wetness in his eyes, could not help admitting that for all their backsliding his comrades had come at once as soon as they heard the call of the Service. Even the blind Asa came trotting along and unerringly took up her correct position—fourth on the left. Everything was done in the proper manner, silently and without fuss. None but the mongrels barked, and they only at a distance; once on the main street they, too, fell silent, for although they had almost forgotten it, they had seen this sight often enough in the past and knew the procedure.

Just because it all happened so easily and calmly, none of the newcomers was scared, no one shied away from the dogs that had suddenly appeared from nowhere to flank the column at regular intervals. Some even dared to reach out and stroke them, and although this did not exactly please the dogs, they tolerated it and did no more than utter a slight growl; they had either grown slacker or more easygoing during the prisoners' absence.

"Hey, Misha!" shouted the young man in rubber-soled shoes, a thin boy with a blubbery, childish mouth. "Look—what service! Have you seen our escort?"

"They must have been provided by the town council," answered Misha. "Or by the factory management."

"Well, whoever sent them, it shows that somebody cares. It would make a good movie shot. Hey, maybe they'd carry our stuff for us?"

"That's an idea!"

And the boy actually laid his pack on Ruslan's back. Perplexed by this novel behavior, Ruslan good-naturedly carried the pack, to the marchers' general amusement, until the boy grew bored with the trick.

"Thank you," he said, raising his cap. "We'll all take it in turns."

The girl alongside him stretched out her hand to tickle Ruslan's ruff. He sidled away, suppressing a growl, and thought how little sense these dimwits had acquired during their long absence. If they really wanted to please the dogs by doing something with their hands, then they could best hold them behind their backs in the manner prescribed by prison regulations.

The people standing on the sidewalks, leaning out of windows or over fences to watch this strange procession of people and dogs, for some reason did not smile, but looked on in gloomy silence. Gradually, too, the people in the column stopped laughing, stopped irritating the dogs by patting them and shouting at them, until finally there was quiet, in which the only sounds to be heard were the regular tramp of feet and the dogs' loud, hot breathing. Right away this silence struck Ruslan as ominous and gave him an uncomfortable feeling that maybe the prisoners suspected something. But what could this be, since they knew all about everything in advance? Perhaps they were regretting their return, perhaps they had changed their minds about going back to the camp and might at any moment break out in an attempt to escape. He glanced around and saw Dick, with his usual sly look on a muzzle that bore the still unhealed scar of his beating; behind him, keeping the regulation interval, trotted the hefty, imperturbable Baikal; farther back, her shoulder blades twitching faintly but rhythmically, Era was jogging along in her place; all of them were busy doing the job for which they were born and trained, and none seemed troubled by any forebodings, which Ruslan found reassuring. He turned and looked ahead to where the street ended at the edge of the town, and the open road started to curve uphill toward the camp. At last he could truly appreciate the meaning of what was happening: they had come back! They had really come back! It was the greatest moment of Ruslan's life, the moment when his star reached its zenith. For the sake of this moment he had endured hunger and homelessness, had warmed himself on heaps of cinders and been soaked to the skin by the spring rains, had eaten mice and taken nothing from strangers; for this moment he had guarded the Shabby Man, and rejected his master when he had shown himself to be a traitor. At this moment he was happy and full of love for the people he was escorting. He was taking them to the bright abode of peace and virtue, in which an orderly regime would cure them of all ills—just as a medical orderly takes to the hospital a patient whose reason has been unbalanced by the importunate attentions of his family. And that love, compassion and pride were vividly expressed in the dazzling smile that was spread across Ruslan's features from ear to ear.

He was still smiling when he turned around, surprised by a momentary disturbance—a muffled growl and a fearful, almost deathly human scream. The smile was still on his face when he suddenly knew he was the most miserable of all dogs, having instantly grasped the import of what he saw. The inevitable had happened. Here, along the town's main street, were all its stores, shops, kiosks and bars—and no one had reminded the returning inmates that they were forbidden to step out of line. There had been no masters present to read out the customary simple instructions; instead of mumbling to a piece of paper about "cellulose fiber factory...," the thin man should have announced briefly and intelligibly: "If you move out of line one pace to the right or one pace to the left ... the escort will open fire without warning...." In the past, the regulations had been read out daily to these dimwits—in fact, every time they were mustered into columns, because by the next time they might forget.

Clearing his throat, Djulbars trotted unhurriedly past Ruslan, accompanied by Dick, leaving Ruslan to watch over the still undisturbed ranks. At the back of the column everything was in confusion: angry barking, the shrieks of people bitten or just frightened, the sound of thumps and wheezing gasps as dogs were kicked in the stomach. Numbly he watched the scuffle in the dust, the glint of bared teeth, the falling bodies, the flailing legs and fists, the suitcases with which the people tried to beat off the infuriated dogs. For a moment he felt a thrilling surge of excitement that made everything around him turn yellow, but immediately the feeling ebbed away again, leaving nothing but sickening despair at the way everything had gone so absurdly wrong. The growls that he could hear told him how it had begun: it was the hot-tempered Cartridge, who always went to extremes. She invariably lunged straight for the throat and brought the man down. Era, of course, immediately joined in; neither of them had the sense to give a warning push to bring the offender back into line with a nudge of the shoulder or forehead, nor would they be content with a simple nip on the leg.... Oh, there were any number of ways of making a man obey without going for his throat!

He watched the affray almost apathetically, concerned only that someone might break ranks. For a while no one did step out of line until suddenly the girl next to the boy in rubber-soled shoes stopped and ran back before Ruslan could prevent her. When she returned and seized her neighbor by the elbow, he seemed utterly stupefied. Ruslan rushed between them and nipped her on the knee. She leaped away with a squeal, which surprised Ruslan; he could not have hurt her, because even in an emergency he had the knack of closing his jaws on a human limb without even breaking the skin. The young man alongside her, who had moved half a pace out of line, had no need of such a reprimand: Ruslan only had to curl back his quivering lips and the boy was already standing in his proper place, furiously offended but also frightened to an equal degree. Ruslan immediately felt he could trust him—he seemed a good boy, who had quickly grasped what he was supposed to do.

Now Ruslan saw an amazing sight: Djulbars running away from the fight. He had a bloody mouth, his piglike eyes were bloodshot, but it was still Djulbars, deserting his post when the situation was not yet under control. Near him was Lux, whimpering as he limped away—exaggerating as usual, since he had no visible injuries. Djulbars on the other hand was not only covered in wounds, but was panting with enthusiasm!

With a nod of his head he beckoned Ruslan to follow him. Together they ran to the corner of a side street, but there Ruslan stopped. And Djulbars stopped, too. It was clear that he was not panting with the thrill of the fight but with exhaustion, that his trembling legs could hardly support his body and he was longing to lie down. Now, with no masters present, he could admit this. Ruslan understood him, but even so he insisted that Djulbars return to the fray. He knew that the dogs would go on fighting as long as Djulbars was there; old, tired and lazy though he might be, provided that they could hear his commanding growl, none of them would dare to retreat. Djulbars could scarcely meet Ruslan's accusing look, while Lux could not tolerate it: forgetting to limp, he bounded up to Ruslan and bit him savagely in the neck. Infuriated by this, Djulbars made a move to punish Lux, but the mongrel jumped back, whining that he had suffered enough already.

Once again the two dogs stared at each other. There was a certain pity in Djulbars's eyes, even though he had never liked Ruslan, who, in his opinion, carried devotion to the point of fanaticism. Now their mutual incomprehension was complete. As Djulbars saw it, they had all had a good scrap and it was time to go home; from now on it was none of the dogs' business, since the masters had long since abandoned their responsibilities. Finally, exercising his right of seniority, Djulbars relieved Ruslan from his post—but in vain: the fanatic was already on his way back to the column. Djulbars watched him go and shook his head sadly. Then, growling at Lux to get lost, he trotted off up the side street and retreated into old age with his regal, leonine gait, scattering drops of his own and others' blood, glad yet regretful that this was his last fight.

Another shock awaited Ruslan: he found the front ranks exactly as he had left them. Surprising though it may seem, a deep-rooted human habit had ensured that the lines at the head of the column remained virtually unbroken: no one had told them to disperse. He ran up and down the ranks, straightening them out and keeping the marchers in line with a warning growl.

The trouble had started outside a bar, but the brawl had already moved across to the other side of the street: there almost all the dogs were fighting as a pack, attacking, dodging and maneuvering, occasionally jumping up onto the sidewalk to catch their breath, while the tail end of the column continued to march on, treading on those who had fallen down in the scuffle. Three men leaned calmly on the railings of the porch outside the bar, each holding a mug of yellow liquid in one hand and in the other a small skinned fish. They were local people, and of no interest to Ruslan; what was more, they politely moved aside to let him pass.

Strangely enough, he saw neither Era nor Cartridge, who should have been in the thick of it. The rule was simple—while some attacked, the others kept the rest of the flock in order. But although he could not hear the inseparable pair among the dogs in the melee, he did notice a gap in a nearby fence, through which the trail of their scent disappeared. Obviously the marchers had wrenched out several fence posts with which to beat Era and Cartridge, and this had only helped them to make their escape; it was, of course, useless to imagine that Era and Cartridge could be beaten into submission with mere fence posts—nothing less than beams or cart shafts would suffice. Yet the fact remained that the two most hotheaded dogs, who had started it all, had also been the first to run away. A little beyond the gap in the fence, Ruslan could see some of their handiwork: a man who had either crawled there, crossing the ditch unaided, or had been carried there by his friends who had then sat him down against the fence. He had been well and truly savaged. He was clutching his throat with both hands, blood was seeping through his fingers onto his torn white shirt, his eyes were glazed and a deathly pallor was creeping over his face, visible even through his suntan. Era and Cartridge had clearly been beaten off very quickly; otherwise the man would not even be sitting up.

Man and beast stared into each other's eyes. At first the man struggled to decide whether he was delirious or whether this white-fanged monster really was no farther away from him than the width of the ditch, then his eyes filled with despair and entreaty, and large drops of sweat began running down his face. The animal merely gave him a look of sullen reproach: have you forgotten, he was saying, that no guard dog ever attacks a man on the ground without being ordered to? He waggled his ears, as a signal of peace, and turned away. At that moment a woman flew past him, wearing a flowered dress and holding something white. She was hastening to the wounded man and did not notice Ruslan, but something that she had seen out of the corner of her eye made her look around. Ruslan's calm and silent approach frightened her more than if he had growled and lunged at her. Slowly teetering backward, eyes wide with fear, whispering to herself, she leaned her back against the side wall of the bar, while her hands continued mechanically to twist her strip of white cloth into a tourniquet. Was she really hoping to beat Ruslan off with that piece of plaited material?

He was about to walk past her when a savage blow winded him and threw him off his feet, hurling him up against the same wall. Only because he fell against the woman's legs was he able to stay upright. With a wild scream she started lashing him with her tourniquet; this only served to reassure him that he had nothing to fear from her.

Which of these three men, converging on him with furious looks and grasping heavy pieces of luggage, had kicked him in the stomach? Anyway, it didn't matter. The time had clearly come for Ruslan to intervene. He weighed up the three men in a swift glance. One had been bitten in the hand and had only just staggered to his feet again after being knocked down by Baikal. Still only able to shuffle forward, he had not yet fully recovered his senses. The second man—short, stocky and tough, with a blank round face and one swollen eye—was really dangerous; men of his build were hard to bring down, and because they thought slowly they were not usually in a hurry to retreat. The third was the boy in rubber-soled shoes, the same boy with the sulky, blubbery mouth who had made Ruslan carry his pack. Ruslan had excused him for one violation of the rules—why was he trying to make trouble again? Why were the three of them advancing on him, when only one of them was any good in a fight?

Ah, that was why! They were talking to the woman in the flowered dress to encourage her and were going to her rescue. This was ridiculous, because Ruslan had no intention of harming her; she had merely been standing between him and the ditch, which she had not dared to jump over because that would have meant turning her back on him. How stupid the whole thing was!

He advanced toward the men, teeth bared, his weight shifted slightly backward onto his hind legs. Not expecting this attack, two of them backed away. The squat man stood his ground. Ruslan had calculated on this, and crouched in preparation for a leap.

He did succeed in flooring his stocky opponent, but the man had time to swivel and meet Ruslan's onslaught with a shoulder that was as hard as mahogany. It was a mistake to try biting that shoulder, but he had already started to get mad—if only the man would at least shout! Silently and deliberately the squat man freed both hands and gripped Ruslan by the neck. Everything around him became blurred and a chill began spreading through his body. Helplessly scrabbling with his claws at the squat man's chest, he fought and strained to tauten the muscles in his neck, as oblivious to the blows on his back as if it had turned to wood. He felt nothing until a heavy, solid object with a sharp edge struck him on the forehead between the eyes. As it hit him, though, the backpack frame must also have hit his adversary's fingers, because the man's grip relaxed, enabling Ruslan to wrench himself free, gulp down some air and leap back toward the wall of the bar. The woman in the flowered dress was no longer there.

The column had disintegrated and turned into sheer chaos, into a nightmarish shrieking mob gathered on the far side of the street, from whence Ruslan could still hear the voices of three or four dogs. Yes, there were now only three or four, headed by Baikal. He was a good fighter, Baikal, levelheaded, brave and strong, who never panicked, took a long time to tire and was able to infect others with his calmness—but if only Djulbars had been there! They might all have fallen in the struggle, but they would have tamed the flock.

The three men, who were far from beaten yet, were advancing again. The squat man was on his feet once more, calm and silent, not even holding his shoulder—and Ruslan realized that the situation was serious.

A fourth man had appeared from somewhere and was now moving forward ahead of the others. He was wearing an army tunic, army breeches and boots, and he had a short, straw-blond forelock. From the way he walked, his hands spread wide to grasp Ruslan's collar, and from the way he talked—with a sibilant whistle in his voice as he called out in an affectionate but authoritative tone: "Here, good dog, come to me, good dog"—Ruslan guessed that the man had been trained to handle dogs. The old Ruslan would probably have obeyed this soldier, but not the Ruslan who had taken poison from the hand of his treacherous master. A master who was in league with the prisoners was an enemy many times more dangerous than the prisoners themselves.

Out of the corner of his eye Ruslan saw Dick, sneaking

away behind a man's back, between another person's legs, limping across the street toward a gateway. He was holding one bloodstained forepaw off the ground. Infuriated, he would turn and lunge at his tormentors, but each time he forgot about his paw and fell whimpering to the ground. Several people were beating the blind Asa as she cowered helplessly against a fence—surely she had not been fighting, too? The soldier could see all this—and yet he could still say, "Come here, good dog!"

Only at the very last instant did the soldier give up his attempt to cajole Ruslan. As he flung up his elbow in defense, Ruslan sank his teeth into it and brought the man crashing down into the dust. The soldier squirmed and groaned, feebly attempting to push the dog away with his other hand; he would probably have given in had he not been surrounded by his companions, who were kicking Ruslan in the ribs, pulling at his tail and ears. Ruslan hung on and would not let go of the man's elbow, although he now realized that it was useless. He was unlikely to intimidate them even if he bit through the soldier's bone: the only effective move was to get one of them by the throat. Seizing a moment when the other men seemed to hesitate, Ruslan suddenly leaped away from the soldier in order to catch his breath and size up the situation.

His despair at seeing Alma escape through the gap in the fence was only slightly relieved by the fact that her mongrel companion managed to make a worthier exit, taking a hefty bite at the leg of a prisoner who was whacking him with a fence post. If only that white-eyed mutt had been properly trained, he would have known it was useless to go for a man's leg when he had a stick in his hand.

Where the crowd was thinner, Ruslan caught sight of

Baikal, trying to counterattack against two men who had chased him up a side street and were roaring with laughter as each tried to jab a fence post into Baikal's mouth. That was it: Ruslan was alone. He alone must now reassemble this whole maddened, yelling, disobedient herd of lunatics, and even though he had lost all hope of escorting them all the way to the camp, at least he must hold them here until the masters arrived—surely they must be coming soon!

His rear was protected by the wall of the bar. No need to worry about the three men leaning on the railing; they had not changed their pose the whole time, and were simply watching the affray with drunken amazement. Nor was there anything to fear from the woman leaning on her spade behind the fence and frowning sorrowfully all over her brown, sunburned face. Most dangerous of all was the soldier, who was now sitting up in the dust, pressing his bitten elbow to his stomach. That man obviously knew something about the Service and might, filthy traitor that he was, encourage the others and instruct them in the proper tactics, but fortunately he seemed too concerned with his wound. There remained the low fence, which he could jump over in case of need, elude pursuit and return to the attack from another direction. That was his only hope. Meanwhile the crowd had formed into a semicircle and was closing in on the lone Ruslan—a crowd of angry faces, each person clutching either a stick or a heavy piece of luggage.

He growled—angrily, menacingly, savagely, to show that he was in no mood to joke but ready to kill or to die himself—and advanced on them, baring his quivering fangs. They stopped, but did not retreat. No, he had not managed to intimidate them. Again and again he made rushes, first at one, then at another, and they dodged him, held up their packs like a wall, then lunged at him from the side and jabbed him in the flanks with fence posts, or purposely exposed themselves to his attack, taunting him with their proximity, in order to smother him with a canvas jacket or a raincoat. He knew that they were purposely wearing him out while the others, behind their backs, could run away in all directions.

He must get to grips with at least one of them and give him a proper trouncing. This was what he had been taught by the masters, by the Instructor and by the men in gray overalls: better to go for one man properly than to make halfhearted attacks on four or five. By now, though, he was seeing the world through a yellow film: the grass and the dust were yellow, the blue afternoon sky was yellow, as were the men's faces and his own blood trickling from the cut on his forehead—and in this state he had no more dangerous enemy than himself. He picked out the boy in rubber-soled shoes, who for some reason angered him more than any of them, although he was standing well out of the way and only watching. Perhaps, in fact, he chose him for the very reason that an attack on this boy would act as more of a shock to the others and restrain them for longer. When two men made a grab at him, Ruslan outwitted them, slipped between their legs and hurled himself at his victim.

Ruslan leaped, his long body fully stretched, his bare-fanged, bloodstained muzzle thrusting ahead with ears flattened. But even while he was in the air he sensed that he was going to miss his target. Because he could now only see with one eye, the other being covered with blood, he had misjudged the distance and jumped too soon. The boy gave a wild, inhuman shriek, and an instantaneous, purely animal instinct made him double up his body. Ruslan brushed him with his stomach, somersaulted over his head and crashed to the ground. Immediately, before he had time to get up, he was thumped on the head by two fence posts, and another man, running up unseen, took a swing with all his strength and brought down a heavy trunk with metal-reinforced corners onto Ruslan's back.

After a blow like that, what power could lift a stricken animal to his feet? Fear of being hit again? But they had stopped hitting him, and he sensed that if he stayed lying down they would not touch him again. The urge to protect his young would have made him get up, but Ruslan had no offspring and he had never known that feeling. He did, however, know another feeling, one that had been taught to him by man: duty—which we, who hardly know the meaning of the word ourselves, had imprinted on his consciousness—and it was duty that obliged Ruslan to raise himself up.

His mouth was full of dust. Nearly choking, he spat it out, then with an incredible effort straightened out his forelegs and sat up. He could do no more, and it was not this fact in itself that horrified him, but the thought that the Enemy might guess that he was helpless. They had moved in quite close now, near enough for him to get at them, but he did not move and only shook his head, growling hoarsely.

"Leave the poor devil alone, boys; don't tease him anymore," said the soldier. He was still sitting on the ground, tearing at his sleeve and binding up his elbow. "He's only doing his duty."

"Who's teasing him?" said the boy indignantly. "You call *that* doing his duty? Filthy beast!"

"He is nothing of the sort," said the soldier. "That's what he was trained to do, so he does it. If only everyone did their duty half as well. You and I can learn a lesson from him." He grinned though wincing with pain. "And I wouldn't mind having a dog like that myself."

"But he's just attacked you..."

"That's exactly why I'd like to have him. Don't go near him! You're not his master."

The soldier began tying his torn sleeve into a knot with the aid of his teeth. The boy came up to him.

"Can I help you? They've called for a truck. There are about twenty people wounded."

"Well, if a truck's on the way someone will help me anyway, so you needn't bother. As for the number of people wounded, my friend, you don't go around broadcasting it to all and sundry. You just say: 'Casualties were sustained.'"

His head drooping, Ruslan kept himself in a sitting position by exerting all his strength on his forepaws. Now and again he gave a growl to remind people that he had not capitulated, but he could not understand what was holding them back—didn't they realize that he could not get up?

This was how the Shabby Man found Ruslan: sitting in the dust, bloodstained, wretched yet terrible. His flanks rose and fell, steaming. His hind legs were splayed out on either side in such an absurd, unnatural attitude, and his spine was bent in such an odd curve that it convinced the Shabby Man that the dog's backbone must be broken. In this the Shabby Man was wrong, and the mistake was to prove fatal for Ruslan.

"What did you have to break his back for?" asked the Shabby Man. "You didn't need to do that. Ah, you young people—love a fight, don't you? And it has to be to the death."

"Yes, they did get a bit excited," said the soldier.

"You can't talk!" said the boy to the Shabby Man, his indignation flaring up again. "You didn't see what happened!"

"No matter what happened," said the Shabby Man, "I know for sure that you didn't have to smash that dog's spine."

"We both know that," said the soldier.

As the Shabby Man approached Ruslan, wanting to stroke him, that terrible head was raised, the lips were curled back and the teeth bared. Usually this was sufficient warning to induce a human to understand and retreat; besides, the Shabby Man needed reminding that never for one moment had he ever been Ruslan's master.

The Shabby Man needed no such reminder. He stepped back into the ranks as quickly as he could—or rather, into the place where the ranks had once been.

"I see you haven't forgotten," said the soldier with a grin. "You remember the rules, don't you? Only one other thing—hands behind your back!"

The Shabby Man did not answer him.

The boy, looking sad and thoughtful, also seemed to understand the situation.

"Well, what's to be done with him?" he asked, glancing around in perplexity. "We can't just leave him like this. He must be taken to a vet."

"You're joking," said the Shabby Man. "What vet can mend a broken spine?"

"This is a job for the weight lifter," said the soldier. "Hey, weight lifter!" he called out to the squat man. "You still feeling mad at this dog? Get a spade and finish him off. It's got to be done, see? Orders are orders."

The squat man gave Ruslan a swift glance from his puffy little eyes and walked over to the fence. At once the woman obediently handed him her spade and turned away, but through the big holes that had been torn in her fence she could still see everything that was happening.

The squat man turned the spade this way and that. It looked like a toy in his huge, muscular hands, but he had no doubt never had to kill before; he was clearly unwilling, and not sure how to do it.

"Why must it be done like that?" asked the boy. "Doesn't anyone here have a gun?"

"No," said the Shabby Man. "No one in this town ever had a gun. It was forbidden."

The crowd made way for the squat man. Ruslan was no longer growling and had hung his head again. He saw the legs in their dusty boots planted wide, the shadow of the spade flickered past him as it was raised, and suddenly Ruslan was seized with fury—this time, though, the fury was his own, and not a response bred by human conditioning. He knew that there was no one to restrain him now, and he knew that he was beaten. But an animal will always fight for its life to the bitter end; no animal ever licks the boots of his executioner. Thrusting out his head, Ruslan lunged toward the spade and caught the iron in his teeth.

Although the pain was terrible, he had the satisfaction of seeing the squat man's face turn pale, his eyes fill with terror and confusion.

"Hey, he's a tough one!" said the squat man, wrenching the spade free and smiling guiltily—no doubt in the same way that he smiled when one of his weight-lifting exercises failed at the first attempt. "What the hell am I to do with him?"

"Well, whatever you're going to do—do it," said the Shabby Man. "You've got to finish him off. He can't live—he's a goner."

Flushing red in the face, the squat man raised the spade again. He approached from Ruslan's blind side, and let out a hoarse grunt as he brought the spade down in a slantwise blow. Turning his head at the sound of the grunt, Ruslan just caught sight of the flashing metal—dull and cold, like the bottom of an aluminum feeding bowl that has been licked clean....

Then the two of them, the squat man and the boy, picked him up by the forelegs and dragged him to the ditch, leaving an intermittent trail of red, caked dustballs. But the owners of the nearby houses protested vigorously at having a carcass left to rot outside their windows, so they had to drag the body a long way beyond the last house and fling it down the embankment made by the bulldozer.

With it, they also threw the spade, stained with saliva and blood.

6

WHEN BLIND ASA HAD LICKED CLEAN THE wounds on Ruslan's flanks and his back and the terrible deep wound behind his ear, she howled a lament for him, instinctively lifting her sightless head toward the sun. Then she went away, certain that Ruslan would never regain his senses.

But regain them he did. It may seem improbable that with a horribly bruised back, with all his weight on his forelegs, his hind legs only scraping along the ground, he should have climbed up the stony-sided embankment and dragged himself all the way to the station. It seems improbable, unless one knows how obstinately, purposefully and unerringly any stricken animal will find its way to the same place where in the past it has endured suffering and recovered. No doubt if Ruslan had been fully conscious he would not have done this, but his mind was clouded now and in his inward eye he could see only one thing—that secluded corner beside a stone wall, between the public lavatory and the garbage cans, where he had recovered from being poisoned.

The sultry afternoon had driven all the people indoors, into cool shuttered rooms where the wooden floors were sprinkled with water. There was not a living soul to be seen. Stupefied by the heat, the yard dogs were dozing in their kennels or under porches, and none of them raised a bark when Ruslan crawled along the wooden sidewalks past their homes. As twilight approached, however, the dogs awoke and began to show an interest in him. It was they, in fact, who forced him into full consciousness. On top of all his misfortunes, he was fated to undergo one more ordeal, and the most humiliating of all: to be tormented by the mongrels of the town, those Buttons, Blackies, Busters and Fidos that he had once so despised. Unaware of what he had done to wound their pride, he had forgotten that peculiarly nasty streak in the canine nature (perhaps explicable in these wretched little creatures by their defenselessness and their frequent maltreatment by humans) that makes them gang up and attack another animal when he is weak and defeated—and the bigger he is the more gusto they put into their persecution. Strangely enough, however, many of their attacks petered out ineffectually or seemed much weaker than he had been led to fear by the fury that seethed in their voices. Somehow they failed in their cowardly attempts to settle accounts with Ruslan. Some strong, resolute companion, keeping pace with him on his blind side—perhaps it was Alma or Baikal, but he could no longer recognize them by their voices—was beating off all their attacks or taking the brunt of them on himself, and the rest of the little dogs' aggression was diverted into snapping and biting each other. Eventually the whole pack was driven off by some kindhearted passerby. The mongrels took to their heels willingly and in a high state of self-satisfaction; all they had wanted, in any case, was to get one bite at him apiece, and afterward the tales of their valor would grow large enough in the telling.

A little later, as he was hauling himself painfully across the station square, Ruslan saw his defender, and his immediate thought was to wish that he had stayed and died at the bottom of the embankment. The dog who had defended him against that vicious rabble was Treasure—that same squat, potbellied little mutt, whose help only yesterday he would have disdained as beneath his dignity.

Treasure stayed with him to the end of his journey. When Ruslan's hind legs proved too infirm to move unaided into the narrow space of his chosen refuge, it was Treasure who performed that service for him. Ruslan was now protected on three sides, and he hoped to be able to defend himself from the fourth side. Treasure could go now. But he still sat there, resting, occasionally giving a violent shiver and whimpering with persistent fright and the pain of his many bites. He wanted an answer to the final question that he was asking Ruslan with the sad, reproachful look in his eyes—something on the lines of, "Why did you do it, brother?"

Ruslan dismissed him with a shake of his head—the head that so terrified Treasure, with its blood-caked eye—and Treasure understood that it was no use putting the question: Ruslan himself did not know the answer. He also knew that he must leave at once, because what was about to happen to Ruslan was more terrible and more important than anything else he might want to know, and that no one must be present to see it. He backed away, his hairs standing on end with fear, and as soon as he had turned the corner around the trash cans, he ran off with a howl that nothing could stop.

Sometimes you may have seen a little dog running down the middle of the street in the gathering darkness, uttering now and again a muffled whine as if through clenched teeth, and apparently running away from something, even though no one is chasing him. It is almost as though he is running away from himself—or from the edge of an abyss over which he has peeped from curiosity or lack of caution, a gulf into which no living creature should look, and from whence he has brought back a secret to make him shiver with cold even in the warmest, safest place of refuge. Treasure had discovered the merest inkling of that secret, yet he was condemned to shiver as with cold, to spurn his food, to ignore his mistress's call, and to crawl into the dimmest, darkest hole, to thrust his nose into the corner and screw up his eyes. Yet even there the thread linking him to Ruslan would not be broken; even there he could not hide himself, and he would go numb with terror as he listened to his swelling, thumping heart, not knowing that it was beating in time to another heart—and that so it would be until that other heart stopped beating. Only then would the link be snapped, allowing him at last, exhausted and in pain, to sink into the oblivion of sleep.

The sound of Treasure's howl fading into the distance was not the last noise to disturb Ruslan. For a long time he could hear footsteps and voices as they approached and died away again, the banging of trash-can lids right above his ear, and the clank followed by a gurgle of water each time the lavatory cistern was emptied. Each sound made him freeze and hold his breath, but by the mercy of fate no one noticed him. Even if anyone had seen him, they would have taken him for a heap of gray rags or some other garbage.

He was waiting for night, when the place would be quiet and deserted, for there was something that he longed to recall, some fleeting memory that he must catch. He did not know what would happen to him by morning, yet he had nevertheless prepared himself for some event; he felt that he was due to return to a certain place: was it perhaps to that black oblivion from which he had once come? And gradually time began to turn backward for Ruslan.

His days in the Service flickered past—most of them as identical as the barbed-wire fence posts or the rows of huts— his turns of sentry duty, his escort duty, his chases and fights. He recalled them all as colored with the yellow of anger and aggression, and everywhere he was a captive—whether on the leash or not—for at no time had he ever been free or on the loose. He wanted now to return to an animal's first joy— to freedom, which he never forgot and to the loss of which he was never reconciled; he hurried on and on until finally he reached it, and saw himself in the spacious enclosure at the breeding kennels, saw the pink and brown-spotted teats of his mother, a famous prizewinning bitch, and his five brothers and sisters fighting and tumbling over one another on the soft bedding. Through the wire-mesh fence that formed the outer wall could be seen bright greenery, yellow sand and a dazzling blue sky, but they never noticed the fence itself and it never occurred to them to wonder what it was for. Two men approached from the other side of the fence, opened the wire-mesh gate, and in walked his master. He entered with another man, already familiar to them, who often came in with food for their mother and swept out the kennel with his harmless broom. This was the first time that Ruslan saw his master: young, strong, well-built, wearing the beautiful dress of the masters, with his handsome, godlike face, his terrible flashing eyes filled, like saucers, with cloudy blue water, and for the first time he felt an unaccountable fear that not even the closeness of his mother could assuage.

"Choose one," said the man with the broom.

Squatting down on his haunches, the Master looked them over for a long time and then stretched out his hand. Immediately Ruslan's five brothers and sisters crawled toward that outstretched hand—submissive, whining pathetically, shivering with fear and impatience. Their mother, delighted and proud of them, prodded them forward with her nose. Only Ruslan, his hackles rising, crawled away growling into a dark corner. It was the first time in his life that he had growled, in fear of the Master's hand, whose short fingers were dotted with a sparse growth of red hairs. The hand passed over all the other puppies and stretched itself out to him alone, picked him up by the scruff of his neck and carried him out into the light. The dread face came nearer—the face that he was to love, and then to hate—and grinned, at which he growled and struggled, wriggling all his paws and his little tail, full of anger and terror.

It was in this position that he came to know his name, which was not the name that his mother had given him to distinguish him from her other children—to her he was known as something like "Yrrm."

"What's his name in the register?" asked his master.

The man with the broom came closer and stared.

"Ruslan."

"Why 'Ruslan'? That's usually a name for retrievers. I thought of calling him Jerry, but we already have a Jerry. What the hell, Ruslan will do.... Do you hear what your name is? Why are you squirming so much? Don't you trust your new master?"

With two fingers he opened the puppy's mouth and inspected his palate.

"Seems like he's a bit of a coward," observed the man with the broom.

"Much you know!" said Master. "He's mistrustful, the little brute. Just the sort to make a good guard dog.... Ah, temper, temper! Bite my finger, would you?" Laughing, he gave Ruslan a painful slap on his little bare belly and put him down separately in a corner. "Feed up this little fellow for a bit longer. And you can drown all the rest. They're just asslickers—not worth shit."

Without even looking at her other puppies, the mother gathered Ruslan alone to her side. The five that had been rejected were put into a bucket and carried away, to be replaced by five greedy foster children, whose teeth had already started to come through and who hurt her teats; she accepted them uncomplainingly and licked them all over, gazing devotedly into Master's face.

Why hadn't she attacked him and bitten him? Seeing himself again as a helpless little puppy, he was still puzzled by her serenity, her untroubled brow. Horrified, Ruslan had tried to make a dash to save his brothers and sisters, only to be struck down by a blow from her heavy paw. What kind of pact existed between her and the Master? There must have been some grim truth she knew that made her obediently submit to the murder of her children—for when a mother animal's young are taken from her, it can only be to destruction.

That grim truth had been revealed to him today—when he had been knocked down and saw the three men advancing on him with faces twisted with hate; when the backpack had struck him on the head; when the spade flew up; and when the Shabby Man had said, "Finish him off." Never, never was the hatred stilled in the hearts of those dimwits; they were only ever awaiting their hour when they could vent it on you—and all because you were doing your duty. The masters were right: in every human who was not of their number there lurked an enemy. But were even the masters his friends? Only the Instructor, who had eventually turned into a dog, had been a real friend—and what had he been barking on that frosty night, to the howling of a snowstorm? He had said: "Let us leave them. They are no brothers of ours. They are our enemies. Every last one of them is an enemy!" So everything that had happened today had, after all, been foreseen by that wise she-dog, his mother, doomed as she was in exchange for her food to bear and suckle aggressive, mistrustful creatures for the Service. Was that why she had shown no distress when her puppies had been removed from her—because she knew that the five who were carried away in a tin bucket were going to the better fate?

... Every animal, when stricken by misfortune, crawls away to a place where in the past he has found refuge in which to endure suffering and recover. This was not the reason, however, that made Ruslan crawl to this place; he knew that this time he could be cured neither by Asa's healing saliva nor by the bitter herbs and plants whose scent he always smelled whenever he was unwell or injured. A wounded animal lives for as long as he wants to live; but now he had sensed that there, in the place where he had been before, there would be no murky cellar, no beating with the leash, no jabs with a needle, no mustard, nothing, no sound, no smells, no alarms, only darkness and calm—and for the first time he longed for that. He had nowhere to go back to. His humble, imperfect love for man had died completely; he knew no other kind of love, he was unfitted for any other form of existence. Lying in his stinking hideaway and sobbing with pain, he heard the distant hooting of locomotives and the clicking wheels of approaching trains, but he had no more expectations from them. Even his erstwhile visions, which had once brought him such delight, now only gave him pain, like a bad dream that leaves a sense of shame and unease on awakening. He had learned enough in his waking life about the world of humans, and it stank of cruelty and treachery.

IT IS TIME FOR US TO LEAVE RUSLAN, AND THAT indeed is now his only wish—that all of us, who share the guilt of what was done to him, should finally leave him and never come back. Any other thoughts that may arise in his brain (which is beginning to suffer from inflammation) will be beyond our comprehension—and it is useless for us to expect enlightenment.

It was, however, Ruslan's fate that even in his last hour the Service did not leave him. It summoned him at the very moment of his crossing to the other shore—calling upon him to make some last response. At that hour, when the Service was being betrayed by the truest of the true, who had sworn without reserve to give their lives for it; when it was being renounced and forsaken by ministers and generals, judges and hangmen, by hired spies and voluntary informers alike; when the very standard-bearers were trampling upon its despised banners—at that hour the Service sought for a prop and stay, called for at least one whose loyalty had not faltered—and the dying soldier heard the call of the war trumpets.

He thought that his master had returned—no, not his previous master, the Corporal; it was someone else, who had no scent and was wearing new boots, to whose smell he still had to grow accustomed. But the hand that he laid on Ruslan's forehead was firm and masterful.

... The buckle clicked, releasing his collar. Stretching his arm toward the distance, his master pointed to where the Enemy was. And Ruslan, breaking loose, raced away in that direction—in long, springy strides, without touching the ground—powerful, free of pain, free of fear and free of love for man or beast. Behind him rang out Ruslan's favorite word, the one and only reward for all his pain and for all his faithfulness:

"Get him, Ruslan! ... Get!"

THE NEVERSINK LIBRARY

AFTER MIDNIGHT
by Irmgard Keun

978-1-935554-41-7
$15.00 / $17.00 CAN

THE ETERNAL PHILISTINE
by Odon von Horvath

978-1-935554-47-9
$15.00 / $17.00 CAN

THE LATE LORD BYRON
by Doris Langley Moore

978-1-935554-48-6
$18.95 / $21.50 CAN

THE TRAIN
by Georges Simenon

978-1-935554-46-2
$14.00 / $16.00 CAN

**THE AUTOBIOGRAPHY OF
A SUPER-TRAMP**
by W. H. Davies

978-1-61219-022-8
$15.00 / $17.00 CAN

FAITHFUL RUSLAN
by Georgi Vladimov

978-1-935554-67-7
$15.00 / $17.00 CAN

THE PRESIDENT
by Georges Simenon

978-1-935554-62-2
$14.00 / $16.00 CAN

THE WAR WITH THE NEWTS
by Karel Capek

978-1-61219-023-5
$15.00 / $17.00 CAN

AMBIGUOUS ADVENTURE
by Cheikh Hamidou Kane

978-1-61219-054-9
$15.00 / $17.00 CAN

THE DEVIL IN THE FLESH
by Raymond Radiguet

978-1-61219-056-3
$15.00 / $17.00 CAN

**THE MADONNA OF THE
SLEEPING CARS**
by Maurice Dekobra

978-1-61219-058-7
$15.00 / $17.00 CAN

THE BOOK OF KHALID
by Ameen Rihani

978-1-61219-087-7
$15.00 / $17.00 CAN